Richard was born and grew up at Horton Farm and enjoyed the rugged life of a farmer's son growing up in Shropshire. When he left school, he at first worked on the farm alongside his father before going to the RMAS Sandhurst as a TA Officer Cadet. He then joined the Regular Army and served with the 10th Bt Gurkha Rifles in Hong Kong and Borneo and then the Light Infantry in Northern Ireland and Germany. When he left the Regulars in the mid-1990s, he again worked on the farm for a few years before joining the Police in which he now still serves. Richard remained a Reservist and has seen operational service in Kabul, Afghanistan in 2002-03.

Very happily married to Louise to whom *Chasing Crows* is dedicated and in memory of his parents. Richard now runs the farm with his wife and three children where they run a small Aberdeen Angus herd and breed Shire Horses.

Dedicated to Louise and in memory of Mum and Dad.

Richard Jones

CHASING CROWS

AUSTIN MACAULEY PUBLISHERS™

LONDON • CAMBRIDGE • NEW YORK • SHARJAH

A CIP catalogue record for this title is available from the British Library.

ISBN 9781398493735 (Paperback)
ISBN 9781398493742 (Hardback)
ISBN 9781398493759 (ePub e-book)

www.austinmacauley.com

First Published 2022
Austin Macauley Publishers Ltd®
1 Canada Square
Canary Wharf
London
E14 5AA

Table of Contents

Chapter 1
St Anne's Shropshire 2013

Crows can live for up to 60 years in captivity and over 30 years in the wild. They mate for life and the old men of the fields always warn not to shoot the crow as it will bring bad luck… The farmer has one pair of crows to his farm.

The old man was now in his 75th year and he felt it! He was perched halfway up the church spire, an ugly old church built in mid-eighteenth century, the result of a rift between the village and the church authorities. He had been warned when he had bought the place that it was cursed but he dismissed such nonsense.

"Granddad George, are you okay?" George's grandson stood on the bottom rung of the ladder peering up at him, concern etched upon his face. The younger man had been raised by his granddad since his own father had been killed when he was an infant.

George clung to the ladder, ignoring the calls from below. He felt faint; there was a weird light at the edges of his vision. George had never feared heights or indeed feared much in his long life, but he was afraid now. He looked up into the sky, past the dragon weathervane he had had to erect himself as he couldn't persuade any of the farm workers or villagers to scale the steeple.

Past the weathervane, George gazed into the cobalt blue July sky. Cloudless and empty and yet there was in that blue expanse a presence. The weird light around his vision continued and he knew he needed to get down from the spire fast. For once leaving the tiling job undone. It was never his way to leave a job half-finished, but he rapidly descended the ladder down to the flat turret roof of the church.

"I am fine, Charlie!" George shouted down, lying to his grandson. "Just the wrong nails for the tiles. I will have to go back to the farm. Anyway, you get off; I had better get home to your nan. I thought you were going out tonight anyway so get off early."

Charlie knew that he was dismissed, there was something odd or different about the old man, but he could not put his finger on it. Anyway, he had his own problems. He was only back on leave from his Regiment based on Salisbury Plane and he hadn't had time to catch up with his girlfriend much to her annoyance as his granddad had immediately grabbed him to help with the Church roof. The young man didn't need to be told twice and jumped in his Jeep and drove off down the green lane leading to the main road and the village.

George was alone, the swallows whizzed around the church spire and roof, rearing their second brood of the year. Nesting in the same spots that they had used since he was a boy and beyond then back generations to when the church had been built during the Napoleonic Wars before even George's ancestors had farmed the land.

The old man struggled down the steeple ladder and then across the flat roof of the tower before going inside and slowly climbing down the stairs inside the Church itself. Once on the ground outside, he calmly walked to his clapped-out old Land Rover and climbed behind the wheel. The lights in the sides of his vision were still there and he felt faint. He knew he needed to get back to Rachel, his wife, but he just needed to rest for a moment. As usual, he had rushed out of the house that morning not thinking of any lunch, in order to get to work on the Church spire.

He had called Rachel many times during the day from his mobile, but she had failed to pick up and he feared the dementia that he tried to hide from their friends, family and community was gripping his wife's once beautiful and vibrant mind.

He sat in the 4x4, his mind a blur with what had just happened. He was still struggling and these bloody lights in the corner of his vision would not go.

The inside of the Land Rover was warm and snug. He closed his eyes and drifted off into a deep sleep. A crow flapped down from the church roof and landed lightly on the bonnet of the Land Rover. The crow stared unblinkingly at the sleeping old man sat behind the wind shield. It then flapped away silently.

Chapter 2
The Farm Spring 1942

George was running as fast his young ten-year-old legs could carry him. He had been picking oats in the wheat field with the two newly arrived Italian prisoners of war, Massimo and Fabiano, when they had all heard a loud snort and to his horror he saw the old Ayrshire bull had been spooked by the passing munitions train and had broken through the thick blackthorn hedge into the wheat field they were in. The munitions train had puffed away unaware of the drama it had caused, the driver intent on getting his heavy load of shells from their ammunition dump hidden away on the Ness cliff moor down to the railhead in Birmingham. He would then collect a totally different consignment of prisoners of war, refugees and wounded soldiers to be transported up to the camps and hospitals scattered around the west and north Shropshire area.

At first, the bull seemed somewhat dazed. He had finally escaped the confines of his two-acre patch, and he had fled from that infernal roaring machine that passed his field twice a day. The pain of the blackthorn spikes, so much more painful and effective than the more common hawthorn, began to register in the flanks and under carriage of the bull, enflaming his already short temper. The bull quickly spotted the two men and boy and focused his rage, fear and pain onto them and so began the chase.

Massimo and Fabiano, barely more than children themselves at eighteen, hardly had a word of English between them and the young George had delighted in trying to teach them the rudiments of the language. In the two weeks since they had been sent from their POW camp, the three young people had become unlikely friends. Young George found in these two Italian older boys a kindness and friendship he did not yet have with his own older brother, the truculent Idris.

The three lads began to run from the bull, back along the wheat field towards the safety of the farm and the sheds. Despite it being early June, the ground was still damp from a heavy spring shower and the lads splashed through the muddy puddles with the two Italians shouting unintelligibly in Italian.

"Salvare! Maschio toro! Salvarel Maschio toro!"

The Italian lads were city boys plucked from relatively comfortable urban lives in the suburbs of 1930s' Rome to go and fight a war they did not understand in the deserts of North Africa. Now here they were in a cold, wet land where no one understood them or wanted to know them except this young English eight-year-old and all of them running from a crazed bull.

The more they ran and shouted the worse became the Ayrshire bull's temper and fear. A small bull, he had always been a source of concern to George's mother, Ruby, but the bull threw such good calves and there were rarely any calving issues that George's dad Tom had kept him but confined him to what should have been a safe field for the Summer. It had always seemed to Tom the smaller the bull the nastier and more aggressive they are. A bit like humans, the 6' 4" tall Tom had once grumbled to his 5 foot wife Ruby!

Tom looked up from his lathe in the farm workshop. He could see the young Italians shouting and scuttling to the edge of the wheat field. Massimo, the larger of the two Italians, was pulling along young George who was now plastered in muck and the bull was gaining upon the fugitive trio fast. Tom grabbed his long pitchfork and began running to head off the bull as the youths reached the edge of the field, gesturing to the Italians and George to make for the nearby orchard. Tom began hollering and bawling at the bull to try and draw his attention away from the fleeing boys.

The bull took no heed of the flailing arms of the farmer running towards him from the buildings. His blood was up, and he was closing in on the small boy fast. Massimo's grasp of George had slipped and, intent on self-preservation, the two POWs had scrambled up into the nearest apple tree.

George, unable to reach high enough, turned to run towards the brook, 100 metres off to his left, darting left and right as he ran with the bull now bearing down on him.

Suddenly, the bull halted, a great black figure had rushed past George who, head down in his frantic dash had not seen that Boleck, the great broad Polish evacuee who had been walking in the meadow with the massive farm Shire horse had immediately leapt upon the great horse's back and rode without hesitation up towards the charging bull.

There was only one creature on the farm that the bull feared and that was Storm the Shire horse. The feelings of antipathy between these great beasts were mutual. The Shire stallion loathed this aggressive little bull and nostrils flaring raced toward the brook with the Polish giant urging him on.

The bull stopped and for an instant considered his options. The great Shire was closing fast, and the boy had disappeared into the reeds near the brook. Knowing he was beaten, the bull turned and this time it was his turn to flee.

Boleck, an accomplished blacksmith and horseman, skilfully used the Shire stallion to coral the bull back to the yard where a visibly relieved if shaken Tom held a shed gate open and they quickly secured the now exhausted bull.

George's mother, Ruby, having watched in horror from the farmhouse had run down to the brook and gathered the terrified George into her arms and was leading him back to the house. The two Italians climbed sheepishly down from their toe holds in the apple trees as Boleck walked the Shire back to the pasture.

Boleck, a man of few words, despised the Italians who to him represented the evil fascist axis that had destroyed his beautiful country and caused him to flee with his fellow free Polish guerrilla fighters, leaving his sweetheart and his father's thriving blacksmith forge. He and his fellow partisan had retreated into the forests around Gdansk and then when all was clearly lost to Poland took the evacuation route south through the Balkans to the allied ports in Greece and then by ship to England.

Whilst he served his internship as the authorities formed new free Polish army units Boleck, along with his fellow Poles, had been sent to work on the farms around his drab intern camp built near Oswestry.

Boleck had been horrified when the Italians had arrived, freshly captured from the North African front and sullenly ignored them.

"Idiotes."

Boleck growled at the dishevelled Italians as he secured Storm back in the pasture field.

Ruby had got the exhausted young George back into the cool of the farm kitchen. She sat him down in Tommy's rocking chair and began scrubbing his muddy face and legs. George began to sob quietly as delayed shock and fear overtook him and the normally undemonstrative and aloof Ruby cuddled her little boy.

"It's okay, little one, you are safe now."

Tommy clattered in and, finding any signs of emotion awkward at the best of times, busied himself on the black stove, putting the kettle to boil to make a cup of tea. His youngest son Gareth, only three but already shaping up into a fine sturdy young boy, came bundling into the kitchen having been busy in the back garden playing with the farm dog, a tired old Labrador called Maggie.

"I told you that bull needs to go," Ruby said without looking up, her soft Welsh voice carrying the cold aloof authority she had inherited from her school master father.

"Ruby, I am not going over this again, we cannot afford a new bull and he throws first class calves. Anyway, it was that bloody stupid train that spooked him. I'll send the bull over to the field next to the church. It is quiet there. You okay, young one?" Tommy ruffled George's black hair. George smiled up at his dad with the worship that a young son often has for his father at that age, when dad can do no wrong. "And how are young mutely?" Tommy turned to Gareth lifting him up and tossing him in the air.

Gareth shouted with delight and soon both boys were wrestling with their dad whilst Ruby looked on in feigned disapproval, but a smile slowly crept across her face.

16

"Right, I need to get moving," Tommy said as he sat up on the mat holding both sons in headlocks on the floor. The lads continued to struggle and yelp as Tommy complained, "I need to get Boleck and the Italians down to the bus stop for the military transport and get to the drill hall for parade. We are going up onto Middletown Hill tonight to light up that decoy fire."

Tommy as a younger man had been a keen Territorial much to his own father's distress. Granddad Bill Jones had fought at the Somme and had been a victim of a German gas attack at Passchendaele in 1917. Despite surviving and returning to the family farm, he never recovered and had died when Tommy was only in his early twenties of a combination of lung disease brought on by the devastation that the mustard gas had wreaked upon his lungs and alcoholism and depression as he had struggled and failed to come to terms with his experiences in the trenches.

Tommy with his young wife Ruby had been left to run the farm and care for his devastated mother Kate who gave up the will to live when her beloved Bill died and followed him to the grave within twelve months.

The TA had provided Tommy with a release and a comradeship he missed on the farm.

The only son Tommy had had a lonely childhood. He had only one sister ten years younger than him, Daisy. Tommy had then been very excited when his father was mobilised to the Western Front in the New Model Army. In 1915, Tommy had been just 15 years old left at home with his depressive mother and baby sister of five years. Tommy had quickly taken to running the small, tenanted family farm and being the main carer to his mother and father figure to his sister. When his father returned home after months in a military hospital in 1918, his dad was a broken man, no longer the ebullient, outgoing, fun dad of before the war but a reclusive angry man taken to drinking and long periods of illness brought on by his devastated, gassed lungs.

It was almost a release when his dad had died of a heart attack during yet another alcohol driven coughing fit in the farmhouse cellar as he sought more wine. Tommy did not know at that point alcohol would ravage his family for generations.

Bill died in 1922. Tommy, then 22, had just married Ruby, a young teacher and daughter of the local headmaster. Ruby's parents had never approved of this black-haired tenant farmer known around the village and country as Mad Tom for his wild eyes and short temper when crossed.

Ruby had been the making of Tommy with her intelligent, reserved manner and very importantly family money, coupled with Tommy entrepreneurial skill. Between them, they were able to take advantage of the breakup of the large agricultural estates in the 1920s' agricultural depression and in 1928, Tommy bought the farm off the local landlord Field Wing.

Tommy with tireless work expanded his dairy cow herd and flock of sheep but also began transporting large quantities of eggs from his chicken flock to the main market in Manchester and later in Birmingham. A move that saw the farm income increase dramatically and allowed him to ride out the general depression of the 1930.

He managed to place the farm on a financial footing that when the crippling Wall Street Crash started to affect the large landowners Tommy's farm and business was unaffected. By 1942, Tommy had become a successful businessman, landowner and farmer with 200-acre farm. He was also happily married and had three sons, 17-year-old Idris, the bubbly eight-year-old George and his little baby boy, three-year-old Gareth.

Idris was away at boarding school and due to leave school that summer and come and work for his father on the farm.

At the outbreak of war in 1939 Tommy, then almost 40, was too old to mobilise and much to Ruby's relief both Tommy was too old to go and fight despite his service in the Territorials and her eldest son Idris was only 15 in 1939. Tommy was however the clear choice to head up the local village home guard and resuming his rank as Sgt he quickly formed an impressive platoon of 35 local farmers, shopkeepers, labourers and miners from the nearby Cruckton mine.

All these men were either too old to join or, like Wilf the farm hand, were held back in reserved occupation to work the farm and go down the mines. That said, a great number of the older men had seen active military service in the trenches and brought a great deal of experience, some of it very bitter to the small band of Home Guard soldiers.

Tommy's unit, the Westbury Home Guard Platoon's main tasks included assisting the military police with the transport of POWs and refugees from their places of work on the farm and mines back to their camps and security at the many airfields scattered around the county. Another vital role of the Home Guard was to set beacons on the nearby hills to draw the night sorties of the Luftwaffe away from their designated targets in Shrewsbury and further north, Manchester.

The beacons would, it was hoped, attract the attention of the Germans who sought out the munitions line that crossed Tommy's farm and led to the ammo dumps at Nesscliff.

Leaving his young boys sprawled on the kitchen floor, Tommy sprang up. Still a very fit man despite his 42 years, he bounded upstairs and changed into his Home Guard uniform.

Ruby still made no reply and continued to prepare a large mutton stew for the dinner that would feel both the family and the two farm workers, Alf who had worked the land around Horton Farm all his life and Tommy had effectively inherited Alf from his father when he had taken over the farm. Alf's son Wilf who had followed his father into agriculture and also worked for Tommy.

Tommy re-entered the kitchen freshly shaved and smartly turned out in his pressed Army fatigues and polished ammo boots.

"Tommy, you know we need to speak to Alf and Wilf soon," Ruby said as Tommy prepared to leave.

"Idris leaves school next month and turns 18 in August. You know Idris is coming to work at home, but he will be eligible to be called up and we only have one reserved occupation position on the farm."

Tommy had been dreading this conversation, young Wilf had worked full time on the farm for four years and as Alf and Tommy were too old to be conscripted, Wilf had been able to take the reserved occupation position on the farm. However, with Tommy's eldest son Idris coming of age, it was either Idris (a keen young farmer himself) or Wilf that had to be mobilised.

Ruby had no qualms about telling Alf or Wilf she was having the reserved occupation post back for her eldest boy, but Tommy was a softer hearted soul and was racking his brains to think of a way he could keep both boys at home safe on the farm.

"Yes, yes, okay. I will speak to them tonight after supper. I need to speak to them about getting the sheep in tomorrow for dipping anyway."

With that, Tommy was gone and Ruby watched him through the kitchen window as he climbed into little grey van and drove off down the yard.

Tommy knew he needed to sort out the reserved occupation position but did not have the heart to take the position from Wilf. He pulled up at the barn and shouted over to Boleck who was putting the Shire away in the stable. Boleck looked up silently then he gestured to the two young Italians who were lolling on some straw bales wearily while they waited for Tommy to collect them all.

Boleck climbed wordless in the front alongside Tommy leaving the Italians to struggle into the confined space in the back of the van.

Tommy didn't know what to make of any of them.

Boleck, a massive young man, hardly ever spoke but when he did, he had a good grasp of English despite his thick Polish accent. He was a great asset to the farm with his skill with both the horses and his ability to work metal. The young Italians were city boys and totally unsuited to the rigors of 1940s' English farming. Also, their lack of any language skills made every task set them a massive effort. Still, they cost next to nothing, and Tommy knew it was his duty to employ and keep them. Any pair of hands, no matter how soft, would be a help during the approaching harvest when he had lost so many of the normal working lads from the village who were now called up to the Army.

The Ford van bounced down the farm lane that led to the main road. There were still puddles from the late spring rain and, although the days were now long, there was still a cold bite to the air as evening wore on. At the junction with the track and the main road into town Tommy pulled over allowing Boleck and the Italians to climb out and stand waiting at the bus stop. The Home Guard corporal assigned with escorting them back to their camp was already waiting alongside the military green bus, an old civilian bus requisitioned by the Army and painted olive green.

"Evening, sarge." The corporal grinned. "You off to the drill hall?"

Tommy, still sat at the wheel in his van, grimaced.

"Yes, Mike, when you have dropped these chaps off. I will see you later."

"Yes, sarge!" came the crisp response and with that all four men climbed into the bus. The driver, another Home Guard corporal, turned the key in the engine and it roared into life and trundled off along the North Road heading towards Ness cliff way and the intern camps. Horton farm stop was the last of their collection points and the bus was now packed with a motley crew of Italian and Romanian prisoners of war and male refugees from Poland. the Baltic States and other Eastern European countries overrun by the Nazis. There were no Germans as the Nesscliff Camp was deemed too low security for German POWs.

Tommy turned south towards the village and the drill hall. The spring evening was rapidly turning to twilight, and he needed to get the platoon up to Middletown Hill before nightfall to light the beacons.

The Luftwaffe would fly over the quiet rural country of Shropshire using railway lines and known landmarks to guide them towards the factories and docks of Manchester and Liverpool to the northwest.

The numerous Home Guard detachments stationed across the rural Shires of England had many tasks aimed at freeing up regular and conscripted troops to train and fight.

Only the year before a household in the Coton Hill area of Shrewsbury had failed to keep the blackout and with an eerie accuracy the Germans had dropped a bomb wiping out three houses and households in the street. Now the bombing runs were less frequent as the Nazis fought for their lives in Stalingrad and post the Battle of Britain, but the threat was still there, and the grim silhouettes of German planes still remained an all too frequent nightly horror for the British public.

Tommy pulled up his van just as the Westbury village church clock struck 7 pm. He was outside the village hall which now doubled up as the night drill hall for the Westbury Home Guard.

"Good evening, Sergeant Jones." The elderly Fielding grinned. Colonel Fielding, now in his sixties, had fought at the Somme and, as was common place in the First World War had been the Platoon Commander in the King Shropshire Light Infantry. He had fought alongside Tommy's dad but had been invalided out with a shrapnel wound to his left leg that left him with a permanent limp.

Fielding's family had once owned thousands of acres in Western Shropshire around the villages of Westbury,

Alberbury and Yockleton but following the Wall Street Crash and the subsequent agricultural depression Fielding had been forced to sell off a number of his farms that he tenanted out.

The Horton Farm had been one of his farms, but Fielding had been happy to sell it to Tommy as he had always a great affection for the wild youth son of his old comrade who he watched helpless as he collapsed into himself after the war.

"Good evening, sir. Sorry I am cutting it a bit fine tonight, no excuses for bad admin on my part." Tommy grinned.

"No problem, but let's get cracking, I want the lads up Middleton Hill pronto! It will be dark in an hour and Fritz will be on his way."

With that both men hurried into the drill hall where the detachment was already formed up.

"Right, lads, let's get to it," Tommy shouted. "Corporal Hare, get the truck started, the rest of you file into the back. Boss, are you joining us?"

"No, thank you," Sergeant replied to Fielding, "I need to get some intelligence reports finished for HQ. You get the chaps up there. C Det has built the fire today so it should be straightforward!"

With that, the Colonel limped to his office and shut the door.

Tommy walked towards the truck, the soldiers had already climbed up and were sitting back-to-back on the central bench inside the canvas covered truck. Tommy slammed the back board up and clipped it shut. He then trotted around and climbed into the passenger seat next to Cpl Hare the local publican and landlord of The Red Lion. "All set, Tom?"

"Yes, let's get going, John." With that, they drove towards Middleton Hill, tonight's designated target for the Luftwaffe!

John Hare had known Tommy since they had been at the local school together as infants. They had grown up together in the village and were very close friends. Both had acted as best men for each other at their mutual weddings and John was Tommy's eldest son Idris's godfather. John and his wife Jill had one child a young 17-year-old girl called Claire. John had worked as a farm hand for many years but, a bright man, he had accumulated enough money to invest in the local Red Lion pub with the financial help of Tommy and had now been its landlord for ten years. John was a committed socialist.

"Old Uncle Joe has turned these Kraut bastards back at last, Tommy!" John began as Tommy settled in next to him and they drove the truck towards Middleton Hill. The one thing Tommy and John disagreed on was politics.

"Yes, mate, it is great that the Russians are pushing those bastards back, but my Polish blacksmith hates the Communists as much as the Fascists. His village was overrun with Russians in 39 and he is not the kind of bloke you argue with!"

"Tommy, the Russians were trying to secure their borders against Hitler. Anyway, the Polish should have been happy to be part of Soviet Union. I only wish we could have socialism here in England."

"Bloody hope not, John! What about the King, and old Churchill would never allow it."

"We will see, Tom. Anyway, we're here now!"

Tommy leapt down from the truck as John parked her up in the lay-by. As soon as engine stopped, Tommy dropped the back boards. "Come on, lads, it's a good 20-minute hike to the top of the hill and it's starting to get dark." The troop, a motley crew of farm workers, miners, publicans, schoolteachers and a postman joined up in the ranks and began a double march up the track to the summit of the hill.

Cpl Hare drilled the men up the hill whilst Tommy went on ahead. The path was rutted but easily passable and Tommy, quickly reached the summit and met up with the Cpl from B Company home guard, a farmer from Welshpool who had been left to guard the beacon.

"Thanks, mate. I will take over now," and the B Company corporal hurried away. It had been a cold long day and he needed to get home for his tea. As he disappeared into the woodland, Tommy took some time to take in the view and to orientate himself. He could hear his squad double marching (a mixture of running and marching as a squad) up the track through the thick wood of oak and ash. Cpl Hare was berating them in his normal good-natured manner. "Come on, you slovenly lot," John called only to be told to piss off and wind his neck in. The Home Guard, unlike the Regular and Territorial Army, was an eclectic mix of individuals, some with war experience in the Great War, some ex Regular soldiers, but whilst they had a rank structure, they were very often civilians in uniform and had to be handled as such. Both John and Tommy understood this and ran a happy unit.

Tommy knew the unit moved as fast as the slowest man and considering that was Pat Greaves the postman, a 52-year-old ex-Private from the First World War with a limp caused by shrapnel and a pot belly caused by beer, he reckoned he had ten minutes to take in the lie of the land.

To the west where the sun was beginning to dip into a red glow stood the great Snowdonia Mountain Range. They were already turning pink in the pre sunset glow. Nestling at the bottom of the hill to the west lay the village of Welshpool and the Welsh border. This was where the B Company Home Guard was from and where their Cpl had hurried away too.

Turning north, Tommy could see the Nesscliff Plain leading onto the bleak Wixhall moss, a large area of peat bog and moorland. At Nesscliff, he could see the intern camps, rows of brown Nissan huts huddled together surrounded by imposing watch towers and wire fences. Inside the wire he could see the POWs milling around before they were corralled into their huts for the night. He knew somewhere amongst the melee would be his two Italians. Massimo and Steffane. Boleck would be further north in the camp at Wixhall moss designated for refugees.

Beneath Nesscliff in vast bunkers were ammunition dumps buried into the earth and well camouflaged. The railway line ran from the camp and munitions dumps arched toward the moor and through Tommy's farm to the east. There, it continued in an easterly direction towards the medieval market town of Shrewsbury and beyond to the city of Birmingham.

Tommy's eyes rested on his home farm Horton. He knew Ruby would be cooking a late tea for him, Alf and Wilf.

Ruby would have put George and Gareth to bed. The house stood out proudly, a three-story Georgian manor house built towards the end of the eighteenth century. Whitewashed and unique the house stood amongst the brown stables and sheds of the farm. The train line ran just to the north of the house and to a mile to the south of the house stood the church of St Anne's on the boundary between Tommy's land and the remaining estate of Fielding.

In the church yard stood the massive Oak planted in 1816 by Fieldlings great grandfather, planted the year after Waterloo to commemorate the victory over Napoleon's Grande Armee and to remember the men under Colonel Fielding's Command who fell in the melee including the Colonel's second son. The Oak known as the Waterloo Tree was now almost 150 years old and towered over the church roof competing with the church steeple for height. Even from this distance of about five miles, Tommy could see a pair of crows had nested in its highest boughs. To the south of Tommy's vantage point ran the Long Mynd range of hills. Tommy was torn from his reverie by the grunting and puffing arrival of his squad led by a very red-faced Cpl Hare.

"Time behind the bar is not doing you any good, John." Tommy laughed.

"That as may be, sarge, but at least I'm fitter than bloody old Greaves. I have left him to walk up. If we wait much longer, the light will be gone."

"You're right, mate, let's get cracking, and come on chaps the light's fading fast."

"John, get a watch on the south just over the brow of the hill, keep an eye on the crest of Caradoc, that's where they normally appear from."

John ran off passing the puffing and wheezing Greaves who had just reached the summit and disappeared into the wood line on the south side of the hill.

Tommy and five other men began walking around the beacon, lighting the bundles of dry straw left by B Platoon earlier in the day. In a very short time, the beacon roared into life and the men fell back instinctively from the raging heat and light. To their west, they could see other similar beacons flickering into life on the barren hills and mountains of North Wales and Snowdonia. To their northeast, again beacons flashed into light with the setting sun this time in the cold damp Wixhall moss to the north of Shrewsbury.

The fierce heat of the beacon drove the platoon back to the safety of the tree line. All the men's eyes were drawn in some prehistoric fascination to the light of the flames dancing and crackling in the gloom. Suddenly, the light of the evening had vanished and whether it was the fire or Tommy's imagination he felt surrounded by a feeling of dread. He found himself suddenly looking in terror away from the beacon to the east and his beloved farm where all he held dear were waiting for his return.

"The bastards are on their way, Tom," bellowed John, a good 100 metres to the south of the beacon. Tommy and the rest of the men automatically started looking to the south and sure enough saw the grim silhouette of a flight of six planes, moving steely determination towards their beacon.

Over the crackling fire, they began to hear the distant drones of the Walter Krupp engines of the six German planes.

"We have them," John shouted gleefully from his vantage point. The planes were banking in the cold spring air, clearly visible against the evening light. No longer heading on a true northerly direction towards Manchester they had taken the bait of the beacon, one of many up the Marches counties and they were now heading directly towards Tommy and his men.

"Okay, lads, let's get moving. These bastards will be over us in five minutes. John, get the lads moving. Fritz will hopefully aim off us and bomb the moors thinking we are a camp or town. Let's go!"

The motley crew had done this drill many times and quickly fell into a squad and began descending the hill, leaving their crackling leaping beacon angrily sparking towards the night sky.

Pell-mell, they dashed down the hill, even fat old Greaves put a spurt on helped by fear and gravity. At the base of the hill where their truck was hidden in the tree line was a bomb shelter and the men scurried inside. Tommy waited until all were safety underground and for a moment, he stood gazing up through the Scottish pines and oak trees into the abyss of the sky above him. Then they were there. The noise of their engine's flattening.

"Get the fuck in, Tommy, for Christ's sake," shouted John, hailing his friend into the shelter just as the first bomber overhead opened its cargo doors and dropped its deadly load.

The two men were hurled back into shelter by the blast as the bomb landed in the trees below the summit. The shockwave smashed into them long before any noise came. When the bang did come, however, they were left numb.

The woods were always cleared long before beacons were lit, and it was just as well as no living thing could have survived the flying splinter as large as a man's leg that hurtled around the hill that night.

John and Greaves managed to secure the hut doors and the men huddled together in primal fear, all the banter gone out of them.

The old Somme and Passchendaele veteran Pte Greeves sat with wide eyes as the explosion shook around them as if they had been transported by some hell like machine back to their nightmare lives on the Somme.

Greaves began to quietly sob while Tony tried in his own way to comfort him.

Tommy sat apart from the men, his ears still ringing. He felt a dark fear. Something was awry and he couldn't put his finger on it. Suddenly, there was quiet. The explosions had stopped as quickly as they had begun. The silence was as oppressive as the noise had been moments before.

Tommy leapt up. "Stay there, lads. John with me, let's check to see if they've gone."

They swung open the bomb doors to see orange light dancing in the trees around them as small fires had started in the shattered woodland all around them.

Their own beacon had suffered a direct hit and had been all but blown out on the hill summit which was now clearly visible through the devastated woods.

With no houses within five miles of the hill and the ammo dump ten miles to the northeast, the damage seemed minor to Tommy.

"John, get the lads out and on the truck!"

Amazingly, the truck had survived the onslaught and the Home Guard lads, terrified moments before fell out of the shelter and gleefully boarded the truck.

"Good job tonight, lads, we've drawn the bastards off." Sure enough, they could see the German planes had banked and were already disappearing into the southeast sky.

Probably relieved to have dropped their hell like cargo and be making for home. Slowly, fat rain clouds were rolling in and it began to rain. "Let's go home, lads. Ruby has done a stew tonight and I am bloody starving."

Grinning, John started the engine and began navigating down the wood track avoiding the smashed tree trunks and potholes.

"We will have to get the engineering lads up here to clear unexploded bombs in the morning. This rain will damp down any fires."

"Fancy a beer in the Lion old chap?" John asked.

"Better hadn't, mate, I have an awkward conversation to have with Wilf tonight."

Less said soonest mended and the men drove on in silence. The elation of surviving the bomb run evaporating in the grim reality of day-to-day war.

They finally pulled into the village drill hall half an hour later and they quickly fell the men out while Tommy went in to report to Fielding.

"Sir, mission completed, and I think a complete success."

"Well done, lad, yes indeed. I watched from the church tower with Father Mark, quite a show! The Intel we get seems bloody accurate. I was only told this morning to expect a run and sure enough just bloody lucky two strong platoons between you and the Welshpool lads. I counted six German planes. Just do a report will you on what you saw? I did see one of those bastards drift a fair way east of the hills. I hope he didn't drop any stray bombs, but nothing has gone off that I can see.

Both men went outside to look up at the Middleton Hill. The fires were dampening down in the steady rain. All seemed quiet as though there was no war and good men were not driven to annihilate each other for perverted beliefs.

"Right lad, the troops have all gone to the pub, Cpl Hare has a new batch of mild ale in and I am going to join them. Are you coming?"

"I really shouldn't sir, the wife…" Tommy mumbled.

"Bollocks Jones, I remember your wife when she was in pigtails. Come on, you have earned it and you need a break, it's an order. Anyway, I need to debrief you on tonight!"

The old major grinned at Tommy and he felt a huge surge of gratitude to this eccentric old gent who had been more of a father to him than his own father.

"Come on. Jump in the Bentley," Fielding crisply said and before he knew it, he was sitting next to the old man as he navigated his beautiful oak interior Bentley the 300 metres to The Red Lion.

"Two pints of Old Hen, please, John," Fieldfare called as he entered the pub, "and a pint for each of the Platoon too."

A roar of approval went up from the 15 Home Guard men all crammed into the small bar area. The pub was dark with blacked out windows and only small candles for light to comply with blackout and the men had to fight through three curtains of blackout blankets at the door to ensure no light escaped. The pub would be closed down if they did not vigorously comply with the ARP rules.

There was a small fire in the corner of the pub and Tommy collected his and Fieldlings pints, walked over to his old mentor who was slouched good naturedly on the sofa.

"Are you okay, lad?"

Fielding smiled up at Tommy as he placed the two pints on the oak table.

"I am fine, just a bit shaken up, I think we all were up on the hill. Poor old Greaves fell apart in the shelter. The Great

War chaps looked dreadful; they had that devastated look in their eyes that Dad used to have."

Tommy settled down in the chair opposite Fielding.

"Your dad was a wonderful man, Tom, that bloody War broke a lot of good men."

"I know, but I can never forgive him for drinking himself to death."

"Don't be too hard on your father, Tom, he saved my skin in France. I often feel it was a massive blessing me getting shot in the leg. It was your dad who dragged me out of No Man's Land. I will never get over leaving the Platoon over there."

Both men fell silent. Tommy knew his dad had dragged Fielding back to safety after they had both been shot up by a German sniper in No Man's Land.

"Your dad stayed out there through the hell of 16, what he must have been through God only knows."

"I know," Tommy mumbled.

Both men felt a similar guilt that they could not shake off.

"Look, boss. I know this sounds odd, but when the bombers came into view, I had a real strange feeling of dread as if something terrible was going to happen. I just felt something wasn't right, I know that sounds daft as nothing is right in this mad world, but it was something else. As if an evil presence was around us. I do not mean the Germans, something else. Am I going mad?"

"No, lad, quite normal actually. Have you ever heard of the Angels of Mons?"

"No."

"Many of the men in 1914 swore blind that as they were attacked by the Germans at Mons what they described as bowmen or archers appeared over their heads to protect them as they fell back from the German advance.

"The HQ at first encouraged the rumours to lift morale but after the war the stories of the Phantom Archers protecting the British troops were discredited. The Government didn't want supernatural rumours about the Army, but I knew a number of chaps who were at the Mons and swore blind the archers dressed from the time of Agincourt over their heads firing back at the Germans.

"Anyway, the point, whether it is true or not is that real danger and exhaustion can play with your mind, Tom. You look shattered and need a rest. So, apart from going a bit crackers and seeing ghosts what is playing on your mind?"

The old man knew Tommy better than Tommy knew himself.

"To be honest it is Alf and Wilf. You know my oldest lad Idris is coming home from school in July and Wilf has the reserve post on the farm. Ruby is adamant that Idris has that position and Wilf is released for service. I just don't know how I'm going to tell Alf. Wilf is all he has in the world."

"Ruby is quite right!" Fielding interrupted.

"You have kept Wilf out of the war since 39, Alf will be grateful for that. Sadly, you need to look after your own now. Tell them as soon as you can is my advice."

"Wilf has just got engaged to John's daughter, Claire. Did you know that?"

"Makes no difference, lad. Do you want another pint?"

"No thanks, boss. I really do need to get home."

"Okay. I will run you back in the Bentley."

"No need," Tommy replied hurriedly, a drive in the pitch black with the merry major was not something he relished.

"If I cut across the fields, I will be home in 15 minutes."

"Roger that old chap." Fielding smiled. "I'm going to have another with the chaps. I have to go to the Barracks tomorrow morning to brief the Colonel Lucas the Chief of Staff about tonight. I will drop in at Horton for a coffee on the way home and bring you up to speed."

With that, Tommy made to leave. John's daughter Claire was collecting glasses.

"Good evening, Mr Jones. If you see Wilf tomorrow, can you tell him that I will be finished here at 5 tomorrow evening?"

"Yes of course, Claire," Tommy muttered as he struggled to escape through the blackout blinds. It was now 1030. Tommy had left the farm with Boleck and the Italians at 5.30 pm and Alf and Wilf would have got the 50 Ayrshire cows at 6 pm. They would have taken until 9 pm to finish the milking and take the cattle back to the 14 acre next to St Anne's.

Tommy's beacon was lit at about 8.30 pm and the bombing run was straight after that.

"I bet these explosions have played havoc with the cows even at five miles' distance." Tommy inwardly groaned as he strode off across the field of wheat that lay between the village and Horton.

Ruby would have fed his two workmen and they would have gone home to their cottage by 10 pm. Tommy would not be able to speak to either of them tonight to his relief, but he knew Ruby would not let it lie and he needed to sort it out tomorrow.

The rain had become persistent, and it wasn't long before Tommy was regretting his decision to walk across the three fields. He knew the route back through gaps in the thick hedges, but the wheat was already at knee height and the thick green verdant stalks soaked him as he walked along the edges of the fields. Soon he was at the rail crossing and beyond the line lay the bull's pasture field and Horton.

Tom knew Boleck had put the bull on the north side of the farm near the derelict St Anne's to avoid the munitions train.

As Tommy climbed over the style that lay between the railway line and the pasture field that lead to the farmyard, he smelt the thick stench of cordite. The rain continued to pound down on the black railway line bouncing off the gravel and metal. Tommy looked back towards Middleton Hill five miles to his west but the fires from the bombs had been extinguished by the rain. In the intermittent moonlight, he could see smoke still drifting around the base of the hill.

"I must have got a whiff of the fires," Tommy mumbled to himself. But he felt that deep black fear again as he had done outside the shelter.

Suddenly, a crow called out in the night. Tommy almost jumped out of his skin. There, not two metres from him, sat a massive black crow in the bough of an oak tree. It ignored the rain and seemed to stare straight at him. It called again and then flew away.

Tommy pulled his khaki jacket close and proceeded on. So, he scooted straight through the slumbering herd of Ayrshires who did not give him a second glance. They had soon settled down after the bomb run.

Tom bounded over the ditch and opened the back door to the kitchen to see Ruby reading by the light of a small candle next to the stove.

Rather than the warm welcome Tommy had expected, he was greeted by torrent of invective.

"Where on earth have you been? Linda Greaves rang me to tell me Greaves was in a real state after tonight. It was only because of her I knew you were okay! I don't mind you having a beer, God knows you deserve it, but you could have rung from the pub to say you were okay. You can be such a selfish, thoughtless prat!"

The normally undemonstrative Ruby had tears in her eyes and looked dreadful. "I am so sorry, love, I didn't think."

"That's the problem, Tommy, you rarely do think! We watched the bombing run; it was clear as crystal from here. The whole hill seemed to explode and one of those fucking German bastards flew directly over the house! The herd went nuts, God knows I bet a few of the sheep will abort and all I could think of was you blasted to small pieces on that hill."

Tommy sat on the step, he knew from experience he was in for the long haul and Ruby would not calm down for a while. He also knew his best defence was submission.

"Love, I am so sorry," he repeated.

"And, I had bloody Alf and Wilf here for their supper after they had milked. You promised me you would speak with Wilf. I am not sending my first son to fight in this bloody war. They will need to send me first. We have already given Phillip to the bastards; no one else from my family is going!"

Phillip was Ruby's beloved younger brother, a career soldier and captain in the 2nd Battalion Coldstream Guards who had been killed at Dunkirk in 1940.

Tommy realised he had been utterly selfish. Ruby had always doted on her younger brother Phillip and had been overjoyed when Phillip passed out of Sandhurst and into the Coldstream Guards in 1937. That joy had turned to fear as the war approached and when they had received the report that

Phillip had been killed whilst defending the perimeter at Dunkirk while the great majority of the British Army escaped from the German advance. Ruby had been broken.

It took her six months to be able to talk about it and her parents became even more reclusive.

"I am so sorry, love." Tommy took the now sobbing Ruby in his arms. "I absolutely promise to sort this out first thing."

"Get off me, you are soaked." Ruby pushed him away and left the kitchen.

Tommy was alone in the warm kitchen and his clothes had started to steam. He stripped off his Home Guard kit, heavy olive-green fabric, bloody uncomfortable when wet! Tom hung his kit around the hot stove and sat down in his pants to eat his stew, left by Ruby on the stove. It had been a very long and eventful day.

The following morning was a clear and bright day. The rain from the night before had cleared away and the farm literally shone in the late spring dawn. Tom had got up with the boys at 6 and had headed out with young George to get the cattle in. Ruby still monosyllabic from the night before. Ruby had silently made them both a cup of tea then busied herself with young Gareth.

Tom knew he would not be forgiven or spoken until he had sorted out Wilf and Alf.

The sky was a brilliant blue, a steady cold breeze blew from the east but it was a spotless massive sky, and a brilliant sunrise began to creep over the spires and Castle tower of Shrewsbury to Tom's South East. Despite it being June, there was still a crisp coldness in the air. The heavy dew and rain shone on the grass as the Ayrshire cows slowly trudged towards Tommy and George.

Tom could hear Alf, already up, and at the back of the herd driving the cows on with his sheepdog Chamberlain, named after the erstwhile Prime Minister.

The cows did not take much fetching and streamed past Tommy and George to the sheds where they knew they could offload their uncomfortably full udders.

As Alf walked past the father and son, Tommy fell into step with him, George trailing in their wake.

"Morning, Alf," Tommy began awkwardly.

Alf was like many of his generation, a man of very few words, even fewer words than Boleck which Tommy always thought was an impossibility as Boleck didn't speak a great deal of English anyway.

"Arr," Alf responded before spitting putrid mass of chewing baccy on the floor much to Tommy's discomfort and George's fascination following in their wake.

By now, they were at the yard and Alf was tying the yard gate shut. The herd, safely contained and milling around as they waited for Wilf to take them in to milk.

The new electric milking machine brought in by the Ministry of Agriculture droned on remorselessly interspersed with the cows lowing as they waited.

"Look Alf, can we leave Wilf to it for a bit and pop into the workshop for a chat?" Tommy asked awkwardly. He would have liked to take Alf for a cup of tea in the house but could not face Ruby again and had no idea how Wilf was going to react.

George was busy staring at the phlegm lump Alf had spat on the yard floor. "Arr!" Alf responded before wordlessly walking off to the workshop.

Tommy disconcertedly followed him and noticed George begin to poke the phlegm with a stick he had found so grabbed him by the collar of his coat and tugging him along protesting.

The workshop was back down the muddy track the cows had just come up. Alf walked silently in front of the father and son, dressed as ever in his grime covered flat cap and blue overalls. His short stature had always belied a strong man both physically and mentally.

Alf had always worked at the farm and had very much been Tommy's father's man. Unable to fight in the Great War due to having only one lung after a bout of TB as a child, Alf had kept the farm going whilst most of the men had gone to fight and he still very much looked on Tommy as the young lad and not the boss. Despite this, Alf loved Tommy like his own son, a fact that totally passed Tommy by.

The two men walked into the open doored workshop and Alf set about getting the embers from the forge into a lit fire.

"George, run off and see if Boleck and the Italians are here yet, there's a good lad," Tommy said gesturing to the track that led up to the main road and bus stop. It was almost 7 am and the transport should be along any minute.

George scampered off. Any excuse to practice talking to the Italians who were so much more fun than Alf or Dad or indeed anyone on the farm.

Once the boy had gone, Tommy turned to Alf and took a deep breath. "Alf, you know our Idris turns 17 this July and is finishing school and coming home to work."

"Arrr, I do."

"Well, the thing is, Alf, I can't…"

"You want Wilf to sign up and hand over the Reserve Occupation Notice," Alf interrupted.

"That's fine, Tom, I expected you would. I have already discussed it with Wilf, and he is keen to get stuck in as soon as you can release him from the farm."

Tommy was staggered. This was one of the longest conversations he had ever had with Alf.

"Look, Tom, I watched your dad and all my friends go off to fight at the last show and I couldn't go, it left me forever feeling half a man somehow. Wilf understands that and since his mum died, we have become very close. Wilf wants to do his bit really for both of us.

"He is 25 now and has looked into joining the KSLI but I am and always will be grateful to you and Ruby for keeping him out of it for this long. It is only right you keep Idris at home, he is still so young, especially after Ruby's brother catching it at Dunkirk.

"The only problem I have is young Claire Hare down at the pub. She and Wilf have been stepping out for a fair time now and are engaged. She is not keen at all for him to sign up but that's her problem!"

Tommy was speechless, if only he had spoken to Alf sooner, what a lot of stress he would have avoided, especially for Ruby.

"Alf, I am so grateful to you and Wilf."

"Bollocks, Tom, it is we who should be grateful, anyway, if that's all I shall get back to the milk parlour as Wilf will need a hand with some of the heifers."

Without a further word, Alf was gone. Silent tears were coursing down the old man's cheeks unseen by Tommy who was reeling from the conversation he had just had.

"Must get and tell Ruby," Tommy mumbled to himself. But just as he set off back to the house, George reappeared with the two Italians and Boleck.

"Ah Boleck, good morning. Can you get the Italians up to the pasture next to the line? The hole in the hedge where the bull broke through needs fixing and the whole fence needs checking."

"I will do, Tom, but the best man to instruct the Italians is your George," Boleck replied gesturing at George. "The young man has, err, how you say? I know, become an interpreter."

George beamed at his dad, fit to burst with pride.

"*Andiamo fix recinziore*," George said slowly to the Italians who grinned back at the young boy.

"Yes, yes, Italian very good!" Massimo the eldest Italian replied.

"George that is fantastic," Tommy said beaming at the boy. The day was turning into a really good one!

"Boleck, can you set them off?" Tommy grinned and winked at Boleck and with that, Tommy sprang with a new athletic step towards the house and his wife who was staring at him uncomprehendingly from the kitchen.

Boleck then took control of the motley crew of youngsters. He had been thinking overnight as he watched the Nazi bombing raid blast Middleton Hall how these young Italians were really just as much victims of Hitler and his perverted ideas as he was. Boleck decided that the Italians were as much a fascist as he was, and he would try harder to be kind to them.

"Right, come on, you lot, let's get the fencing kit from the shed and load up the Tractor link box."

With that, the four figures trooped off happily to get the tools needed and loaded them up in the small transport box on the back of the only tractor, a little grey Massey Ferguson 35. Once the transport box had six posts and the sledgehammer on board, Boleck turned to Massimo.

"Right, you were in a motorised unit in Africa, right?"

Massimo just stared at him quizzically. "*Que?*"

Boleck sighed. "You drive, yes? And he made a steering wheel sign.

"*Ah, si si.*" Massimo grinned and leapt into the tractor driving seat.

Pronto pronto, Massimo gestured to Stefano to get in the transport box.

"Not you, George, I need you to help me get the horses."

Boleck said, "But tell these two to drive up to the hole in the fence by the railway."

Massimo rewed up the engine and he and Stefano drove off laughing into the meadow and bumping over the ruts towards the far hedge and railway line. Boleck and George set off to the stables as the buzz of the milking machine ground on.

Boleck looked back towards the Italians on the tractor. He suddenly felt a cold chill.

A crow was fluttering wildly over the Italians and Stefano was cursing in Italian and fending the crow off.

Tommy stopped mid-sentence with Ruby and looked out the kitchen window. "That's odd," he said to Ruby, "I have never seen that before."

"What's that?" Ruby said. "That crow attacking the tractor. Never seen that before."

As he watched, there was a sudden massive flash of light from the field. Then all the windows in the kitchen blew in showering Ruby and Tommy with glass and throwing them to the floor.

"Fucking hell," Tommy cursed and leapt up. "You okay, Ruby?"

"Yes," groaned Ruby. "You check outside, get George. I will get Gareth."

Tommy fled outside. The cows were going berserk, bawling in fear. The horses, including Storm the Shire, had bolted, broken out of the stables and fled over the brook away from the smouldering remains of the tractor that burnt in the middle of the pasture.

Alf and Wilf were running from the milking parlour towards the meadow.

"Tommy!" Boleck shouted. Boleck and George had been blown against the stable wall. Boleck had shielded George from the blast and was bleeding heavily from the arms and chest from shrapnel.

George was crying in his arms.

"Alf, Wilf, stop!" shouted Tommy. "No one fucking move till we know what happened."

Boleck had struggled up and stood next to Tommy staring at the shattered remains of the tractor.

"That was a bomb, Tommy, let's get George in the house; there is nothing we can do with the Italians."

Tommy suddenly realised the Italians were nowhere to be seen. With horror he saw a solitary boot with a foot still in it lying on the grass ten metres from the tractor.

"Shit, right Wilf please take George in the house and get Ruby to call the Military Police. Alf help me get Boleck inside."

A crow flapped down on the roof of the stable and stared at them all.

"Christ you survived then," Tommy muttered as he got his shoulder under Boleck's arm.

"What?" said Boleck.

"Not you," Tommy said, "that fucking crow."

George woke up, his mouth was dry and the inside of the Land Rover was hot.

Christ, how long had he been asleep? Must get back. He fired the Land Rover into life and began reversing out of the church yard.

That was the most vivid dream he had ever had.

Chapter 3
Rachel

The crow had successfully hatched a brood of three in the stricken oak tree that overlooked the farm. The higher branches had been struck by lightning many times over the years and the upper bows looked like scorched arms reaching for the sky. The crow's nest was nestled lower in the tree amongst the verdant green leaves and the three nestlings screeched longingly at their mother and father.

George pulled up outside Horton. He still felt really shaken and knew he had not just dozed off in the car. He was very lightheaded and could still not focus properly.

George knew he should be worried. He had not felt right for months now but he had never had a funny turn like the one he had had on the church roof.

He thought of his own father Tommy who had been crippled by a stroke and spent ten miserable years in a wheelchair before finally dying. George put these dreadful memories to the back of his mind and climbed out of the Land Rover. The weather was still warm, but a wind was picking up and blowing through the oak tree that towered over the old farmhouse.

He tried the front door, but it was locked again. Living in the country, they had never bothered locking doors, especially living on a busy and vibrant farm when trusted friends and workers came and went all day but as his beloved wife Rachel's dementia slowly took hold, she had become more and more insular and reclusive. In the past, the kitchen would be buzzing with visitors and Rachel would hold court but now in the late autumn of her years, she would keep the curtains drawn all day and once George had gone out, she would hurriedly draw the curtains and lock the doors of the house. Rachel had been a very bright, outgoing and intelligent woman, the first woman in her family to go to university and a lifelong science teacher. Her intellect made her dementia on one part crueller but enabled her to recognise her condition and go to great lengths to hide it.

George colluded with this, refusing to accept that the woman he had loved all his adult life was becoming crippled.

On the other hand, she fully realised something was wrong with her, and it terrified her. Now six years after she and George first noticed her forgetfulness, she was a shadow of her former self. Now she peered out with her milky blue eyes from under a furrowed brow with a perpetual look of accusation and fear.

"Hello, love," George said as he climbed in through the conservatory window, he had deliberately left ajar. Rachel had again left the key in the door lock making it impossible to unlock the front door.

"I am not doing any Christmas cards. I am keeping my head clear! I am sick of it, George!"

"Love, it is mid-May!"

"I know that! I am just saying anyway, keep the curtains drawn, the neighbours keep peering in and Idris cut down the ivy crawling up the window."

"Rachel, it is a beautiful day; we need to get some sun into the house. Idris was only doing what he thought was best."

The house that George and Rachel had bought up a happy young family in was now falling into disrepair as George struggled to cope with Rachel and her dementia. One of the facets of which was a total inability to cope with any change. To that end, the garden grew wild and the house fell into ruin.

George knew the conversation was fruitless. Rachel continued to watch daytime TV. She used to watch the 24-hour news but now she watched reruns of soaps. Stuff she would never have deigned to watch when she had been well.

"I had a weird experience today, I dozed off in the car and a crow woke me by landing on the Land Rover bonnet. It just stood there on the bonnet staring at me."

Rachel's eyes lit up. For an instant, the distance confusion left her face.

"My mother always said of crows that they were portents of great change, you must never shoot a crow, and it stays with the farm for life.

"Anyway, I am not doing Christmas cards I am keeping my head down."

Rachel had lapsed back into her ongoing demented state staring out at early summer hawthorn blossoms growing in the hedgerows. Rachel quickly got up and drew the curtains.

"They keep looking in George."

George sighed as Rachel turned the volume up on the TV. He got up and left the gloomy room.

George walked into the kitchen, Rachel had lost the ability to cook so George had had to step to the mark as a cook, something that was very alien to a lifelong farmer.

"Rachel, do you fancy going to the Red Lion for dinner?" George called through hopefully.

"No, I do not George, you always want to go out mealing," came the immediate response. "Right, what do you fancy then? I have some soup here or sausages."

"Crow mean big change, George."

Rachel had appeared in the kitchen doorway and George almost jumped out of his skin.

"If you are visited by a crow, it's an omen, George, let's have sausages." Rachel turned on her heel and returned to the sitting room.

"Sausages and mash it is then," George mumbled.

After dinner, a soulless affair, George sat in his chair opposite Rachel. The TV blared out endless reruns of 1980s' detective mysteries. He had extracted Rachel from the sitting room, and she sat sulkily eating her dinner before lighting yet another cigarette, shuffling back to the sofa, parked in front of the TV.

George shrugged and went and sat next to the large black log burner. He had not bothered lighting the fire for a month now but there was a chilly East wind outside. So, he got to work lighting it then settled down with his newspaper. Within minutes, he was asleep, exhausted from the day.

Chapter 4
Korea Summer 1951

George was shitting himself. As soon as he had turned 18, he had left the farm to join up with the local Regiment, the King's Shropshire Light Infantry. Tommy, his dad, had gone nuts and desperately tried to dissuade the headstrong lad but George would have none of it. With Idris at home running the farm with his dad, George wanted to strike out on his own path. His younger brother Gareth having died of meningitis shortly after the war George had found himself smothered by his parents and was desperate to escape the farm. Now, one year later, here he was on a barren hillside in Korea. It was mid-July and his unit was hunkered up near the River Imgin.

George, a relatively experienced 2nd Lieutenant, had been tasked by his Company Commander to take out a fighting patrol along the river up to the Korean settlement at Kungong-Ni to check for any North Korean army units.

"Evening, boss." The dark-haired Sergeant Lewis crouched down next to George. Although he would have only been in his late thirties, Sergeant Lewis seemed very old and wise to the young George. Luckily for George, Lewis had taken the green young officer under his wing when he had arrived straight from training in Sandhurst, to their training base in Fanling Hong Kong. The men were now firm friends.

"So, what was said at the O Group, boss?"

"I need you to build up a model of the river where it bends South of Kungong-Ni, I won't tell you to suck eggs, sarge." George grinned at Lewis. "But I need these two rocky gullies that lead into the river clearly shown."

George had unscrolled his issue map and pointed to the terrain he was describing.

"The Battalion Reece Platoon has set up an Observation Post (OP) on this parameter here on the map and they have sent back reports of North Korean (NK) activity at the river bend. No idea what it is but we need to get a fighting patrol down there. You get one of the lads to put the model together and then get the platoon rehearsing ambush drills and obstacle crossing. I do not want any repeat of last week's fuck up with 6 Platoon, we are better than that."

"Indeed, we are, sir." Lewis grinned. The young buck was coming along well and had earned the respect of the Platoon and the Sergeant, a veteran of Normandy.

"We have been doing river crossing drills a great deal since those two 6 Platoon lads drowning and we have shaken up all our procedures. It was a balls up waiting to happen.

"The weather is on the turn as well boss," Lewis continued.

"There is a storm forecast and although the weather's warmed up, you remember what the typhoons were like back in Fanling last year."

"Roger that, Lewis. Right, get the men sorted. I need to run through these orders and get the updated intelligence picture from the Military Intelligence chaps. We have four hours till we move out at dusk, so you have three hours to get the rehearsals and model done. I will give orders at 1700 hours at Platoon HQ."

The Army always had a one thirds two thirds rule for orders. The young officer knew the mission would be an intricate task. Sgt Lewis would collect together the best ten men for the patrol and ensure the admin was squared away, rations, ammo ensuring no one's gear made any noises as they moved but George would need to navigate the route, select rendezvous points along the route where the patrol would rest and regroup, emergency rendezvous points where the patrol would return to in the case of separation or after an ambush. One of the key issues facing George was the near total deforestation of the area.

George had found himself working with officers from Australia, Canada, New Zealand, India and America in the Brigade and had delighted in learning new skills from the array of different styles. The landscape was unlike that any that George had seen in his native Shropshire. Over the years, the Korean farmers had deforested the hills leaving them bare and disfigured by endless paddy fields built into the hillsides. The mountains were high and reminded George of the bleak unforgiving landscape of the new territories in Hong Kong where he had been stationed earlier in the year just before they deployed to Korea. It was now late April 1951 and the Korean War had been fought up and down the peninsular firstly with North Koreans pushing the South Korean army and its allies almost off the Korean peninsula into a pocket in the Southern most point of the Korean peninsula called the Pusan Pocket. In late 1950, the UN forces had pushed the North Koreans back and had advanced to the Yalu River near the Chinese boarder.

Having firstly pushed the North Korean and Chinese troops almost to the Chinese border the UN Forces were now once again being forced back by overwhelming Chinese military forces and were fighting near the 38th Parallel. George and his unit had deployed in the region of the Imgin River.

As Sgt Lewis left the Platoon HQ, nothing more than a dug out consisting of a hole with two sheets of corrugated metal tin sheet covering it and George's kit and camp bed in the comer next to the radio equipment. The young radio operator, a Private called Cuffley from Gloucester, was asleep on his kit mat. George tapped the young Private with his foot.

"Wake up Cuffers, you're on stage. Ears on the radio and I'm of to speak to the Ml lot."

Ml or military intelligence were collocated with the Company HQ to George's south. George had to get the intelligence brief from the Ml captain, a dishevelled, overweight Irishman called Laddi Stonefeather.

George nimbly leapt from the trench, his athletic physique the product of farm work from an early age. Leaving Cuffley the radio and Lewis briefing the men, George had a few minutes to take in the austere and alien landscape. So different from to the green rolling hills of Shropshire.

George picked his way from his bunker down a well-worn route up to the Company HQ. His Officer Commanding (QC), the gregarious chain-smoking Major Di Lambers, was sitting outside his 9 by 9 tent smoking and gave him a cheery wave.

"All sorted for tonight, young George?" Lambers grinned.

Lambers was a WW2 veteran and had been at Pegasus Bridge on D Day with the Ox and Bucks Light Infantry. He had the relaxed air of a man who had seen it all before and George and all the other young officers in the Regiment worshipped him.

"Yes, all in order, boss." George grinned back. "Just off to get briefed by Stone feather!"

"Oh, good luck old chap, hope he talks sense to you! I need your chaps out by nightfall."

"Yes, boss."

Lambers grinned at George in a knowing way. Both men knew Stone feather was famous across the Brigade as a highly intelligent Irishman a heavy drinker but a staunch Chapel Protestant from Londonderry whose fixed views of the world did not exactly chime well with the easy-going regimental structure of the KSLI.

Stone feather was crouching over his hexamine cooking stove. The wind was picking up and in the hot July Korean wind Stone feather was struggling to keep his matches alight.

"O for feck's sake!" cursed the Irishman. "What Ho Stone feather," George mimicked an upper-class English accent that he knew would inflame the Ulsterman event more.

"Feck off, Jones, you Welsh arse. What do you want you wanker? And stop with the stupid taffy accent!"

Came the warm reply. Nothing that George did not expect. Laddie Stonefeather was a bright man and an excellent soldier, but he was not blessed with any patience and today was not proving to be a good day.

"I need," started George.

"I know what you fecking need, you Welsh idiot!" Stone feather snapped at him.

"Have you got any dry matches? Mine have been soaked by that prick of a corporal of mine when he spilt coffee over my pack. Light the Hexi block and get a brew on for me while I talk you through the patrol tonight."

Stone feather grinned at George and disappeared into his tent where a deeply harassed looking corporal was hastily gathering maps from the Ops Table.

George crouched down and quickly lite the Hexi Blocks. Using his own tin mug, he filled it full of water from his canteen and put it to boil.

"Cpl Liston, could you grab some of Captain Stone feathers coffee please?" he called into the tent. Cpl Liston duly came out of the tent with an issue tin of coffee granules.

"He is a miserable bastard," the corporal muttered. The two men grinned at each other knowingly. Stone feather and Cpl Liston made up the entire Military Intelligence cell within the Battalion and although they bickered incessantly, they were great friends.

Stone feather clattered out behind Cpl Liston as the water boiled and George moved over to his briefing table where the Irishman was laying out a crumpled map. The positions of the Gloucester and Light Infantry Companies were clearly marked with the village of Chonkgong to the North of the Imgin River curving around to the North of the village. Cpl Liston took over making the coffee from George muttering to himself.

"Right, young George."

Stone feather gestured to George to look at the map.

"Look into the map, you can see here we are near the village of Solmatri. You're Bravo Company under Major Lambers is the North most subunit here overlooking

Chanksong. To our right is Alpha Company and to our rear and south lie Charlie Company, Delta Company and Battalion HQ. To our left flank are the Yanks and to our right flank are the Ulster Rifles God bless them a proper Unit and the Belgians.

"I have received reports from our Reece Units based at the south side of the Imgin that large numbers of Chinese and North Korean troops can be seen moving around on the north bank between the villages of Tunjen and Charumel.

"The river is still fordable but take care we do not want any more drownings. You have had your orders and you know what we need to know. In reality, you are on an intelligence gathering mission, but the Colonel is sending you out in a fighting patrol strength in case you meet serious opposition from the Chinese and NK Troops.

"Cross at this point here where the river turns north, I will ensure the Ulster Reece boys guide you to the Crossing point."

Corporal Liston dumped the two mugs of coffee on the briefing table. "Careful for fuck's sake, don't get the map wet, Cursed Stone feather."

Liston rolled his eyes at George and slunk back into the Ops tent. George stifled a grin and studied the map.

"Christ, have you stuck your cock into this coffee, you bastard Liston; it tastes of feet and cheese!"

Stone Feather grinned at George and continued to drink the perfectly acceptable coffee. "Fuck off, sir!" came the reply from inside the tent.

"Okay, George, seriously take care tonight. I have real concerns the Chinks are going to launch another attack and we need to know where this will be. Brigade do not think the attack will be in our sector, but I am not so sure. You have about one hour before you move out, so get your shit in one sock and crack on! Good luck!"

"Thanks for that, Laddie," George replied. "I will be back at 0600hrs tomorrow with a full report." With that, George finished his coffee stowed his tin mug into his webbing and left.

The sun was setting on what had been a fairly uneventful Sunday along the front line. The date was 22 April 1951.

George passed the Padre, a dour quiet man, who was moving between the slit trenches of the troops at 50% stand to. A cursory nod was passed between each man as George hurried on. The humour and banter from seeing Stone feather and Liston had evaporated and in its place George felt a cold fear. Looking out to the north as he reached his bunker, he could see the tiny village of Chocksong and the Imgin beyond. George had carried out numerous patrols in the months he had been in Korea, and he had been in a number of fire fights with Chinese troops but tonight he felt a real feeling of dread. A deep primeval foreboding as if something dreadful lurked beyond the river only one mile north of his position.

As he stared north, a jet-black crow flapped down and landed noisily on the corrugated metal tin that made the roof of the Platoon HQ Dug Out. The crow stared unblinking at George who for a moment was distracted by the bird.

"Boss, the lads are ready for your orders." Sgt Lewis emerged from the darkness of the HQ Bunker. The spell was broken, and the crow was gone. George was back to himself the fear in his stomach was replaced with a grim readiness to get the job done.

Lewis led George to a small hollow in the Centre of the Platoon position, very few trees had survived the duration of the two-year war. The benighted few tree stumps that had survived had long since been chopped down by Military Units defending the south to improve fields of vision and fire. The wood had also been used to shore up trenches and dug outs. The last of the winter snow had long since melted in the early Korean Summer leaving the valley a sad grey desolated expanse of ground with all agricultural activity long since halted by the war.

"Right, chaps, look into Sgt Lewis's work of art here!" George grinned as his ten-man patrol. The group was an eclectic mix of World War 2 veterans, regular soldiers, territorials and reservists called back to the colours and National Service men. Lewis had picked the best of the platoon which included Cpl Metcalf as the senior Cpl. Lewis had served with Metcalf in Normandy in 1944 seven years earlier. Lewis has chosen well thought George as he scanned the dugout.

Nine fit young faces stared at him intently. "Sir."

Sgt Lewis began to number off the patrol to George.

"Private Jervis will to be the scout with Cpl Metcalf. As you know Jervis is a National Service lad but as fit as a Butchers dog, which is apt as his dad's a butcher in Worcester. You will stick with your signaller Private Cuffley in the centre of the patrol with you and I will bring up the rear of the patrol with lance Corporal Nunnerley who will carry the GPMG."

Lance Corporal Nunnerley was a 6.4 feet tall half Jamaican half English lad who had found a home and family in the Regiment when he had escaped the poverty of central Birmingham. The biggest man in the Platoon, he was always first to volunteer to go on any patrol and Lewis looked to Nunnerley to keep the young soldiers in line.

George began to brief the patrol of men.

"Chaps, young Jervis and Corporal Metcalf will lead us due north below the ridge line to avoid being spotted from the valley floor. We will head to the northwest of Chonksong, what poor bastards are still living there will be keeping their heads down, but the stray dogs will give us away if they can."

Dogs in Korea acted as alarm calls and were the bain of any patrol trying to remain inconspicuous.

"We will then cut due north to where the river bends to the north, here." George pointed to the blue ribbon Lewis had used to denote the river on his model. "Hopefully, there will be a standing patrol of Ulster Rifles who will guide us to the ford across the river."

George went on to spell out where they would rendezvous if there was an emergency or an ambush and where to fall back to, should they get separated from the patrol of lost. At the end of the orders, George reiterated to the patrol, describing the actions the soldiers should take if they were ambushed, lost or separated from the patrol.

"Chaps, our mission is to find out what enemy activity, if any is taking place in the area north of the Imgun River in and around Chonksong." He repeated the mission so that it stuck in the minds of the young soldiers.

"Okay, five minutes till we move out. Sargent Lewis do a kit check please."

"Roger that, boss. Right, lads, form up you know the order of march kit on and jump up and down." All six soldiers quietly stood up pulled on their kit bags and Webbing and then jumped up and down. There was not a sound, no tin rattled and no ammunition rounds clanked.

"Good work, lads, Richardson you ready to lead off?"

"Yes, sarge."

"Okay, sir." Lewis turned to George. George nodded and Richardson led the team out of the bunker and into the gloom of the Korean night.

The patrol moved silently between given rendezvous point to rendezvous point. George would direct Richardson and Metcalf to the next landmark and the two soldiers would then carefully pick the route forward. The patrol moved like six shadows towards the silent village and river beyond. As planned, they kept two hundred metres tops the west of Chonksong where tiny candles flickered in the mud brick houses and the muted sound of human activity carried across the long derelict paddy fields to the patrol. Once north of Chonksong, they went towards the river and sure enough a clicking sound came to them from the riverbank. They moved towards the sound and a figure emerged from the Reed bed.

"Evening, lads."

A thick Belfast accent came from the camouflaged face of the soldier standing between the patrol and the river.

"I am your happy Irish leprechaun guide here to assist you this fine evening! I will take you to the fording position."

"Many thanks," whispered George who had moved to the front of the patrol as the other soldiers crouched down while they waited.

George now led the patrol behind the Irish guide as they passed the remaining soldiers in the Ulster Unit standing patrol deep in the reed bed. By now, the moon had risen high in the Eastern sky and the pale half crescent moon light shone eerily of the sparking water. With no light pollution, the stars and the Milky Way were a magnificent if very bright sight.

"Sir," the Irish soldier whispered, "if you look directly to our front, you can just make out a line of small rocks under the surface of the river. The river is only two feet deep all the way across to the far side but be careful as you go the stones are slippery and if your lads lose their footing they could be carried away by the current.

"We have been here since dawn and there has been no movement whatsoever on the far bank which is frankly really worrying as there have been no fishermen or locals at all. That is not normal!"

Sgt Lewis had positioned the patrol in an all-round Defense at the edge of the river while George recced the crossing point. The Sgt then crept up to George and the Irish guide to listen to the brief. The two men exchanged concerned glances.

"Right, Lewis, I will take point now with Liston. You stay with Cuffley and the radio and drop Metcalf back with the gunner Nunnerley. Let's get across the river as fast as possible and regroup on the far side."

Thanking the Irish guide, the two men moved back to their patrol and George silently tapped on Liston shoulder signalling for him to move and follow George. The patrol walked silently into the river following George as the Irish guide returned to his own standing patrol. The patrol moved forward with tactical gaps between each man. The diminutive Liston was soon up to his waist as they forded the 50 metre wide river.

George stood a good foot taller than Liston and the water only reached his thigh. George's mind was racing, planning the move from the north side of the river towards Tungen where Laddie Stone feather had told him there were possible Chinese Units. The water chilled his legs as he waded on. Then he had that cold feeling again. He was suddenly aware there was something wrong. Out of the dark, a bird flew at him.

"Fuck," he muttered as he ducked down to avoid the black crow that seemed intent on attacking him. As he crouched in the freezing water, all hell erupted from the north side of the riverbank. Flashes of light appeared and the water erupted all around him. They had walked straight into an ambush. Liston was hit three maybe four times and fell beneath the water, his body was quickly carried away by the current. George had been saved by ducking to avoid the crow and Liston had caught the bullets that would have killed George.

"Fall back," screamed George. Lewis was wounded in the leg and Cuffley was also mortally wounded the large radio weighing his body face down as he bumped away with the current of the river.

The 'Burp' of Chinese machine guns began firing all along the riverbank to George's front and the local dogs in Chonksong began barking madly. Grabbing Lewis by his webbing, George frantically began wading back to the south bank of the river as Nunnerley and Metcalf gave covering fire. The Ulster patrol also began firing into the North bank of the river. As he dragged the heavily bleeding Lewis up the riverbank, George looked back and to his horror saw masses of enemy soldiers splashing into the river in pursuit. With his radio operator dead George roared to the Ulstermen. "Get some mortar fire down onto the North Bank."

"Already on it," came the curt reply as the remains of George's patrol scrambled into the Irish position. As if on cue, the scream overhead of British Artillery fire to defend the men and the river to their front erupted British mortar rounds landing on the advancing Korean and Chinese troops.

George and Metcalf lifted their head to see the effect of the first volley and to their disbelief saw the Chinese and NK troops still wading through the river despite the devastation around them. Body parts lay everywhere with the screams of the injured mingling with the machine gun fire and artillery rounds. The Ulstermen opened fire but the Chinese continued to advance on their position.

"Fix Bayonets, lads," called George. Lewis lay on his side bleeding heavily whilst the other soldiers grabbed their long World War 2 bayonets. Then they were overrun. George caught a Chinese soldier as he jumped into the Trench and stabbed wildly in the man's chest with his bayonet. George then felt a massive blast on his back, and it all went black.

Chapter 5
Idris

George woke with a start. The log burner had taken well and was burning ferociously, the dry wood crackled angrily behind the toughened glass of the burner door. He must have only been asleep for minutes, but it had grown dark outside as the mid spring day had come to an end.

He could hear the TV still blaring loudly in the snug behind him where his Rachel sat smoking, glued to a TV world she would have shunned before the dementia began to remorselessly close in on her mind.

The kitchen had grown dark, and the shadows were long. His sleepy eyes tried to focus but he knew in his heart of hearts that it was not just an after-dinner nap he was recovering from.

As his eyes became accustomed to the evening gleam, he began to focus on the figure sitting opposite him. The uniform was distressingly familiar to him as were the oriental eyes that pierced the gloom staring unblinkingly at him.

The Korean uniform, drab brown Ho Chi Min jacket, pock marked with bullet holes and brown pyjama style trousers. The face gleamed in the light from the stove, silent in its own agony bearing witness George thought and then the figure was gone.

George sat there, frozen in his own fear and misery. The phantom of the man he had bayoneted to death sixty years earlier still haunting his waking hours.

Rachel was no longer any comfort to him so he went to the only other peace he could find. Pouring a large glass of whiskey for himself and lighting a cigar, he stared into the raging log burner.

"George! George!"

His peace was shattered as Rachel came angrily into the room. "George, your brother's here. He came to the back door staring in through the window. I am sick of it, George. I am sick of it, George. I can get no peace, no peace. I am keeping my head down. I am not having your father for Christmas again I tell you!"

"Dad's been dead these 20 years," muttered George's brother Idris as he manoeuvred himself past Rachel.

"All right, George son? How are you?"

Despite both men being in their eighties, they were still as close as they had been as teenagers decades earlier.

"You look shit, old lad." Idris grinned as Rachel retreated back to her lair in the sitting room.

"How bad is she?" Idris asked George switching to his serious face now Rachel was out of the room.

"She is fine, thanks!" George retorted immediately on the defensive.

"No, she isn't and neither are you, you daft sod. You look like you have just seen a ghost."

"I have! The China man!"

George had always been open with his older brother about his flashbacks. Despite Idris' lack of any military background, he was a great support to George. Idris had stayed at home to

66

farm with old Tommy their father, but the more impulsive George had needed to escape the confines of the farm and Shropshire.

"Well, you're awake now, old chap, and he has gone! Listen. You really need to get Rachel checked out; she has got a great deal worse lately. Even I can see she isn't as steady on her legs as she has been. Is she eating properly?" Idris grabbed a glass and poured himself a whiskey.

"Oh yes, that is the one thing she does do! I know she isn't right, her memory seems to be down to a five-minute loop and she is getting more aggressive. She hit me the other day and she has never done that before, but I am afraid if I make a fuss to the doctor, they will take her away. I am in my mid-eighties; they may well say I cannot cope and put her in a home. That would kill her… And me."

There were tears in George's eyes as he thought of the once beautiful and intelligent woman he married. He needed to talk to someone, he needed to unload.

"She has not been right since Charlie first went to Afghanistan and that was ten years ago."

George was finally admitting to Idris that Rachel was ill and after years of evasion he needed to get it all out, he needed to talk.

"If you think back, Idris, Rachel and I turned seventy when Charlie went to Kabul in 03 and that was his first time away on an operational tour after his basic training and Sandhurst."

"I saw Charlie earlier driving away from St Anne's. Is he back on leave?" Idris interjected absentmindedly, unprepared for George's download.

"Yes, he is. He is out catching up with friends I think, but he will be back later," George snapped, irritated at the interruption.

"Anyway, when Charlie went out there Rachel got really uptight, she kept going on about Ireland and Phillip. I went out to milk the cows on one afternoon thinking she had settled down and when I came back, I found her flat out in the kitchen.

"She had been trying to clean the ceiling and must have fallen off the work surface she had got up on. I have no idea how long she had lay there, about an hour I think, but she had lost consciousness. I got the doctor out and if you remember they took her into hospital. She seemed okay but a fall like that by a 70-year-old woman was bound to do harm. Anyway, they let Rachel come home after a week and she seemed fine. Bit I could tell something had changed. She had gone quiet. She stopped talking about Charlie or indeed anything much and seemed to turn in on herself.

"It has been pretty much downhill from that date. She stopped planning stuff or looking to the future. That was ten years ago and now she struggles to walk, her memory is dreadful! and she is miserable and angry most of the time. I dare not make a fuss with the doctors in case they say I can't cope and put her in a home but the GP, Dr Pursey, is aware. She has tried to get Rachel to take medication and cut down on the fags, but you can imagine how successful that is."

George rolled his eyes and Idris smiled back sadly.

"She is a good doctor that Pursey," Idris said. "She was wonderful with my Rebecca towards the end."

Idris' wife Rebecca had died three years earlier after a long battle with cancer. With no children of their own, Idris had been left alone and in the past three years had grown closer to his younger brother George.

"Look, George, check Rachel doesn't need anything and get your coat. We could both do with a quiet pint down at The Lion. The walk there will do us both good and stretch our old legs."

Idris and George needed each other so George pulled himself up from his chair, drained his whiskey glass and went and looked in on Rachel sitting in the snug.

"You okay, love?"

No response. George walked into the room and looked down at his wife. She had fallen asleep. The TV still blared out a piece on homes under the hammer on ITV3. Rachel lay there snoring with her mouth wide open and a sliver of drool creeping down her chin, her Embassy Regal cigarette smouldering in the overflowing ashtray.

"Christ, what would happen if one of these fags fell on the rug whilst she slept?" Idris was staring over George's shoulder at Rachel.

"Yes. Thanks for pointing out the fucking obvious Idris," George snapped.

"I try to hide all the lighters when I am out. She only seems to smoke as a reflex now, not as though needs to. Often she will light a fag and just leave it to burn out in the ashtray like that."

"You go to the Lion on your own. I'd better stay here; she has been more agitated than normal lately and I want to be around if she wakes up. If young Charlie is down there, tell him to be quiet when he comes home. I know he is on leave and wants to let his hair down, but he woke the old girl up last night when he came in. I love him to bits and it is great to have him back for a few nights but I will be relieved when he heads back down to Salisbury."

George walked Idris to the front door having turned the volume down on the TV. Both men could hear Rachel's snoring reverberate through the old house.

"Take care, George," Idris said looking closely into the worn old face he had known all his life.

"You are doing all you can and this is no longer Rachel, you know that, don't you?"

"Yes, I get that. I sometimes think your Lucy had a kinder end, don't you?"

"Yes, I do, but I miss her dreadfully," Idris sounded back.

"I miss Rachel too," George replied sadly. Idris looked uncomfortable.

"Are you okay to come with me to the cattle market tomorrow? I have got two steers going through the fat cattle ring."

"No thanks, Idris. It's Charlie's last day before he heads back, so I am going to see if we can both get Rachel to come out for lunch. Why don't you join us? We are only going into town somewhere."

"Okay I will. I will call you after the market and see where you are."

"Deal." The two men grinned at each other, and Idris shuffled off into the gloom towards his tired looking grey van.

George went back into the warm of the kitchen.

"You okay, love?" Rachel had woken and was standing in the doorway from the kitchen to the back snug. She was smiling at him.

"You're awake! Do you want a cup of tea?"

"No thanks, George. I am off up to bed. You should too, you look dreadful. We have a long day tomorrow. I am taking a school trip to Chester."

Rachel hobbled past George and began climbing the stone stairs to their bedroom. George shook his head in exasperation. She had been retired from teaching for over twenty years.

He turned the dials down on the log burner to close it down for the night, left one light on for Charlie in the hall and followed his wife's slow progress up the stairs to bed.

Chapter 6
The Cuban Missile Crisis in the
Farm Kitchen Oct 1962

The birds soared high over the railway line, the old crow trying to teach his offspring to swoop and harass a buzzard that had invaded their territory.

The day of the wedding was a miserable grey October Saturday. One of those days when everything was caked in mud, and it never really got light. There was no warmth in the sun and even less in the cold kitchen where Ruby had pointedly refused to light the Aga as the clocks had not yet gone back so it was still theoretically summer. Tom's feet which were a bane to him at the best of times had begun to crack at the heals a sure sign that winter was on its way. It had been raining heavily on the pastures for eight days and the Ayrshires were covered in cold October mud as they walked slowly and painfully up towards the farm from the Railway line field. Idris had finally relented and agreed to bring them in for the winter despite it still being October as it was clear the ground was becoming poached and worn out by the cattle.

The farm looked dark and foreboding as Tom peered out of the kitchen window across the sodden fields towards St

Annes. He and Ruby should have been delighted today. Their youngest surviving son George now in his 30th year was finally marring his childhood sweetheart. Both parents fully endorsed the wedding that had been a long time coming, the whole village was expected to turn up to St Anne's to see the happy couple. The young bride a delightful girl called Rachel the daughter of a popular local Police Sgt She was a stunning young woman in her late twenty. Ruby was happy with her perspective daughter-in-law who clearly had a good brain as well as a pretty face as she was a teacher at the local school. Rachel had met their George after he had Demobbed from the Army following Korea in 53.

"What on earth is wrong with, you miserable sod?" Ruby bustled into the farm kitchen to find Tommy staring morosely out of the window.

"Get cracking, the lads are dressed and ready to go, Idris is practicing his speech in the front room, and I want you to go and listen to it to check it is okay. I do not want any dirty jokes or smut!!!"

"For Christ's sake, woman, I am just listening to the radio, listen, things are getting worse over in Cuba. The Russian ships are heading there now what kind of mad world are we living in? I am just glad Mum and Dad are not here to witness this. We thought wars were over when we beat the Nazis in 45."

Ruby bristled at Tom's tone and Tom cringed inside knowing he would pay for snapping at her. Ruby was never wrong and brooked no back chat which could be incredibly tiresome, but Tom had realised that in a successful marriage or at least one that lasted one of the partners had to surrender and give up. That was (he concluded a long time ago) going to have to be him.

"I knew you should have laid off the red wine last night," Ruby hissed, "it always makes you miserable. Forget World politics for the day, you miserable git, your son is getting married today. If we are all going to die in a Nuclear Armageddon at least let's enjoy today."

"Good morning, both!" A grinning George breezed into the room resplendent in his old Kings Shropshire Light Infantry Service dress ready for the wedding. "Why the long faces, the cows aren't out, are they?" A look of concern crossed George's face as he anticipated chasing Ayrshires through the shit and mud in his Army Service Uniform on his wedding morning.

"Nothing so desperate," Ruby declared. "Your father is concerned that Mr Krushev and Mr Kennedy might spoil today by dropping a nuclear bomb on us. That and he is miserable because he drank too much wine with you and Idris last night down at the Red Lion. Did you have fun on your last night of freedom, my love?"

Ruby smiled at her youngest son, now a strapping man of thirty years whose still youthful features belied sometimes haunted eyes. Today though those eyes shone with a delight his mother had not seen for many years and for that at least she was grateful and happy.

"Come on, Dad, we are all worried about Cuba but there is nothing to be done, what will be will be. Have you spoken to Bolek since last night? Is he going to be in a fit state to drive the wedding car today? He was well away on that Polish vodka, thank God I only had one shot of the stuff, and Idris looks shit!"

"Look, son." Tom turned from the window and the rain still streaming out of the leaden sky. "I want you to know how proud of you we are. I can only imagine what you went through in Korea, and I know you hate discussing it but I want you to realise we appreciate what you have done and how you have come through it. We adore Rachel and both think you make a lovely couple. I am sorry I am a bit down but a day like today should not be overshadowed by this madness in Cuba so I will cheer up and go and check on Bolek. Poor sod has had to milk the cows on his own today as that lad from the village who was meant to help never showed up."

Tom pulled his overalls from the hook on the back of the kitchen door and climbed stiffly into them. The old man walked out into the cold autumnal rain feeling every bit of his sixty plus years.

George turned to his mother. "I feel bad now, I should have helped Boleck with the milking. We almost had an incident in the pub again last night, Mum. I think we need to start avoiding the Lion."

"Nonsense!" Ruby retorted. "John Hare would be heartbroken if we did that. What happened?"

"It's John's daughter again, she has never forgiven Dad for letting Hoag go to war. She is the Land Lady now that old John has retired, and she just spent the night staring at Dad and Idris and me. We really felt uncomfortable. I normally avoid the place, but Boleck had arranged food there. Old John came out to the Bar after a while and she disappeared into the back, probably went to piss in our beers!"

"George don't be so crude!" Ruby scolded. "The girl was heartbroken when Hoag got killed at Arnhem. I have tried talking to her, but it is no use. She cannot get beyond the fact that Idris came home, and Hoag had to go to serve. You know I lost my brother, your uncle, at Dunkirk. We all suffered; your father in particular took the news very badly. He thought Wilf would never forgive him, but Wilf was great with your dad, but the Hare girl has haunted your father and Idris with cold blue eyes ever since. I am sure she would have rejoiced if you had been killed in Korea."

"All right, Mum, calm down, I shouldn't have said anything!"

"It's poor John, her dad I feel sorry for. He and your father were as close as brothers when they were younger. John served in the same Home Guard Unit as Dad and was a great help and comfort when the Germans dropped a bomb on the farm killing those poor Italian lads. I thought I had lost you that day too."

George was really wishing he had not mentioned last night and began to back towards the door.

"Quite frankly, she needs to get over herself," Ruby continued. "It's a bit rich, she turns up everywhere with those cold eyes staring at your dad, that's what has upset your dad not fucking Cuba or the wine!"

"Mum, what on earth has got into you?" George tried to placate his mother. At that point, Idris walked in and caught the last part of his mother's download.

"Morning, all! Catching up on last night, were we, George? I told you not to say anything! My special fan the landlady of the Red Lion? I normally won't step inside the place. The woman is clearly potty and hates me."

"Yes, we know," George cut his brother off. "How is your speech coming along? Let's go through it, I need to give you the ring and run through my lines with you." The two men left the kitchen both worried that their mum may have another outburst and retreated to the relative safety of the sitting room. Ruby sat alone thoughtfully at the kitchen table. She watched the cold October rain dribble remorselessly down the window pain. She could see her beloved husband and old Boleck both in their 60s moving with the ginger care of men with hangovers driving the last of the cows back to the shed to be milked. Although Idris and George rarely took a day off the two older men had insisted neither of the brothers should work today but Ruby smiled to herself as she watched them struggling on the yard. She leaned over and turned on the radio on. Tommy and Boleck still had to feed the cattle so would be another half hour before they were in. Idris and George were laughing and chatting loudly in the sitting room and Ruby was alone with her thoughts. Her eldest daughter-in-law Clara was staying with Rachel's family overnight to help Rachel get ready for the Wedding.

The old long wave radio on the windowsill crackled into life. The news announcer spoke in a clipped British accent.

"The Soviet fleet continues on its course towards the Islands of Cuba this morning. Mr Krushev has made no response to President Kennedy's insistence that the fleet carrying nuclear warheads to the Castro regime turns back. We are aware the United States Naval fleet has taken up position off the coast of Florida and is preparing to bear down on the Soviet ships. The American navy is placing itself directly in the path of the oncoming Russian ships."

Ruby snapped the radio off, grabbed her wellies and coat and went outside into the rain to help the old men.

Chapter 7
Phillip

The Larson trap is a brutal form of bird control aimed at killing Magpies, the thieves of the forest unable to resist the curiosity of the metal cage. The old crow is far too wily to fall for the trap.

George woke with a start. Rachel was shouting at him, and he felt wet. He couldn't move. "George, George, you have wet the bed! George, my love, speak to me!"

George tried to move, tried to open his mouth but he could do nothing. He felt the warm stickiness of his own filth and knew that he had done more than just wet himself. He tried again to speak and began to panic.

The room was dark, and he could hear his dad's old grandfather clock, the one he had bought off Stonefeather years ago when the old family were in financial trouble tolling the hour. *Three am in the morning,* George thought.

There was a rushing in George's ears. He could hear the blood pulsing and his head beating, but the blue lights were in his vision again. The walls seemed to be fluid and appeared to be moving. Rachel was calling him again or was it the voice of his mother Ruby? *Can't be,* he thought. *Mum's been dead for years.*

"Grandad, Granddad." Charlie had rushed into the bedroom wearing his boxers and a t-shirt. "Look at me, Grandad, are you okay?"

George managed to open his mouth and he could feel drool rolling down his chin. He was acutely aware he was lying in his own shit and piss.

"I am okay, son, I am okay," he tried to say but it just came out as a series of mumbles. Then the spots on the wall got larger and began to move, the blue light began to close in around his vision and he could hear Boleck's dog Marley barking and howling in the yard. That dogs been dead years George thought.

Then there were different blue lights on the ceiling. More real lights more concrete if that was possible. He could hear Rachel crying. "The ambulance is here, Grandad." Charlie came into his view again as he stared towards the ceiling. How long had he laid like this. Idris was there now. "You will be okay, George, you have just had a turn that's all. The old familiar face smiled down at him."

Two paramedics entered the room and carefully moved Idris and Rachel to one side. "Can you help us get Mr Jones onto the stretcher?" George heard the Paramedics speak to Charlie who had somehow got dressed.

The blue lights were back again, not the reassuring Ambulance lights reflected on the ceiling but the cold ethereal light that seemed to close in and begin to envelop George. Charlie had gone so had the paramedics. The Korean soldier was there though standing in the corner of the room staring at George. Beside the Korean stood Phillip, George's beloved long dead son and father to Charlie. Philip was a tall strapping young man holding a rifle and bleeding heavily from the head.

"George, George, Mr Jones we will get you to hospital now!"

George managed to tilt his head to the window. There was a black crow on the windowsill.

Chapter 8
Winter in Northern Ireland

The young crow soared with delight. He was free of the nest and his parent's direction. It was a beautiful summer day as he flew over the farm. On the ground beneath him, he could see a man, not the farmer or his wife who sometimes threw scraps of meat into the garden for him. Curiosity got the better of the young bird who glided lower towards the man moving along the hedge line.

Bang.
Falling to earth.
Blackness.

Letter to Mr and Mrs Jones on 20 December 1982 from Major Mark Hardwick 3 Platoon A Coy 2nd Battalion Light Infantry.

Dear Mr and Mrs Jones,

My name is Mark Hardwick and I have the honour of being your son Philip's Company Commander. You will by now have been visited by our Regimental Padre and Major

Crook our family's officers to inform you of the terrible news that your son Lt Phillip Jones was killed in action on 15 December whilst on a foot patrol in the Aughnacloy area of Northern Ireland.

I would like to give you some background to Phillips service here with us in A Company 2 LI and what we are all doing here in the province.

As you both know, we deployed here in October earlier this year and I can say without reservation that Philip was our strongest young leader. Philip had recently returned from a one-year tour of Hong Kong as a trainer with the Gurkha Rifles and had been stationed on the Chinese border in the New Territory's during this time. The skills and experience he bought to us from this posting were invaluable and he fully deserved his promotion to Lieutenant.

His young wife, Suzy, I am informed fully embraced the sometimes lonely life of a Service wife and the Regiment will extend all the help we can both to Suzy and young baby Charlie who I believe turns one this month. I know Suzy will be back with you in the UK and I am writing to her separately. It is a heart-breaking thing to see and young child such as baby Charlie lose his father before he even knew him.

After Phillip had completed his two-week home leave and set Suzy and Charlie up safely in Shropshire, he returned to our Unit and joined me and the rest of the company. We all then deployed to the training base for Northern Ireland Training on the south coast of England for two weeks before deploying to the province of Northern Ireland. Phillip took over 3 Platoon and became my lead Platoon Commander. The men very much respected him and the knowledge and experience he bought from his time on patrols with the

Gurkhas in the Jungle and scrub of Hong Kong were of great use on our patrols around the province.

We flew out to Ireland in Section packets arriving in Belfast in mid-October and collected by unmarked vans by the RUC at Belfast airport. This was both Phillips and my first tours of Northern Ireland and as you can imagine we were both quite nervous.

I have only been with the Regiment for one year so did not know Phillip at all until I met him prior to deployment. I did, however, find him a very mature patient and wise beyond his years and a young man who would have a great future in the Army.

On arrival at Belfast International, Philip, myself and six other soldiers from the company were directed silently by the plain clothed RUC Officers to follow them. They took us to their blacked out unmarked vans in the car park and we climbed unquestioning into the rear of three vehicles. When the doors of the van slammed shut, it occurred to me this might be a kidnap of some kind but Phillip in his unflappable manner assured me this was normal Northern Ireland protocol designed to ensure our anonymity as we arrived in the province.

We were then driven in the dark for what must have been an hour along unseen Irish back roads until we arrived at the camp based in a small border town called Aughnacloy (or auch no joy as the solders described it). I am sure Phillip would have already described the town to you both but it is a tiny one street joyless place, the houses run either side of the main road that runs from Cooks town in the north to Armagh in the south skirting along the River Blackwater which forms the border with Southern Ireland on the west. The population of the town is split between Catholic and Protestant and the town hosts both a Roman Catholic Church, round domed in its architecture and a more pointed spired and square faced protestant church. The churches stand at either end of the town and almost glower at each other from one end of the street to the other. To the east of the town, the land rises up to the hills of Cappa and Cappa moor which is peppered with staunchly republican villages.

Our Battalion headquarters (and I use these military terms in the knowledge that you Mr Jones are veteran of the KSLI and Korea so will understand these terms) is based in a large market town called Dunganon and the company units are spread around the County of East Tyron with our A Company in Aughnacloy with the task of patrolling the border area along the river Blackwater and to man check points both permanent and temporary to provide reassurance to the outlying communities from both faiths that are threatened by the opposing Paramilitary organisations.

You will I hope be aware that in November this year, Philip received a commendation from our commanding officer Colonel Chambers for his cool handling of a potentially explosive and dangerous scenario. A well-known IRA Commander approached Phillip and his Platoon at a static check point. Only one month earlier at a similar check point in B Company's area, a young Irish girl gave the troops a large tin of Quality Street chocolates before driving away. On opening the tin inside the check point, the bomb inside the tin detonated killing six of the ten men section and severely wounding the remaining four soldiers.

Understandably, the whole Battalion has been jumpy ever since that incident, so it is a matter of impressive note that your son Phillip immediately dealt with the suspect IRA.

Commander who is a well-known Sinn Fein Councillor himself. Despite being well known to our security services Phillip treated the man with respect and caution. The Councillor was clearly in distress and terrified. He informed Phillip that he was being followed and had been followed all the way from Dublin in the South. The car that was following the councillor was being driven by a well-known protestant Paramilitary we know as the King Rat. The Sinn Fein Councillor told Phillip that the 'Rat' had been sent to kill him.

A lesser man would have dismissed the councillor and sent him to his fate. After all, we did not owe the man any loyalty and he detested us. However, Phillip knew that a high level assassination within the province like this would certainly deepen Sectarian tensions and the right thing to do was to help this man despite our concerns about him. Phillip thought on his feet and took the Councillor into protective custody. The King Rat was waived through the check point and flagged up to Special Branch. The Councillor was then released to his family once the danger had passed. Bizarrely, the check point troops were given free milk the following day by the Catholic milkman. Unsurprisingly, the soldiers binned the milk when the milkman had gone as a precaution.

I hope this incident gives you a flavour of the kind of leader and young man your son was.

Regarding the incident on 15 December, Phillips Platoon had been tasked to patrol the small hamlet of Cappa Village and the surrounding moorland. We received a tip off from an informant within the IRA that an arms cache had been buried or hidden on the moor at a particular location. This was the conflux of two mountain streams by a burnt-out tree.

I decided to join Phillips platoon to see how they were performing, and we deployed as normal in Wessex Military helicopters up onto the moor at dawn. The weather was clear and bright with a light hoar frost on the ground. Within minutes of the helicopters flying away from our drop off point, we came under sporadic fire. It appears we were being shot at by a single shot sniper firing rounds from over the River Blackwater on the southern side of the valley which of course sits in Southern Ireland. I only became aware of the incoming fire when I heard Phillip directing the platoon to take cover. The wind was howling around us both from the Heli down blast and a gathering storm coming in from the Irish Sea to out east.

Our soldiers are well trained and we quickly dispersed into scrub and woodland cover forming a typical satellite type patrol technique we use here in the province. I was unable to order a return fire as the incoming bullets clearly originated from farm buildings about a mile away across the border in Southern Ireland and we could not risk an international incident with the Irish Police. The best we could do was radio into HQ and flag up the attack so that they could inform the Garde and the Irish army to deal with it from their side. Although I doubt much came of this!

The satellite patrol is very different to the linear straight fighting patrols you, Mr Jones, would have been accustomed to in Korea. The key is that the Command Section with Phillip as the Platoon Commander, the main Radio operator providing communication back to Company HQ a scout and a gunner. Carrying a large general purpose Machine gun known as a GPMG. We would move along a fixed line picking up the rendezvous points or RVs as the patrols move along. The Command Sect will target the patrol objective of the patrol and once completed they will move to a pickup point or PUP. The two satellite patrols move in a revolving motion around the main command patrol again each satellite patrol consisted of a commander a scout, gunner and radio operator who has communication into the Platoon signaller. There are three satellite patrols to a command patrol. The idea is that one of the satellite patrols intercept any paramilitary patrols or snipers they will then neutralise them and the command patrol is protected to carry on with the mission. I have likened the concept to the command patrol being the parent patrol watching three children patrols. In a play park as long as the patrols can all see each other we are unlikely to experience an attack.

Phillip led his patrol northwards, and we began our 12-hour sweep to try and locate the arms cache on Cappa Moor. However, following the immediate attack from the sniper, I was beginning to think we may have been set up by the informant and this was a trap. We as a unit settled into a normal patrol routine and our training kicked in. We climbed high onto the moor overlooking Cappa Valley and the river beyond.

The patrols entered a number of small farm steads, it is noticeable in Northern Ireland that the agriculturally poor land such as the bogs or moors tend to be farmed by the Catholic community's whilst the more fertile valley farms were on the whole held by Protestant families. I am told this is a hangover from when Oliver Cromwell had the Catholic communities removed from the fertile lands in the sixteenth century. When we would enter a farmyard, we would check the silage clamps and haystacks for weapons caches and hides. Due to Phillips upbringing on your farm his knowledge of what was agriculturally normal and what was out of place on a farmyard was vital to the success of our area searches. Phillip would often locate firearms and weapons hidden underneath piles of silage or hay noticing where feed piles had been disturbed when they should not have been.

We found nothing on the day of our patrol so broke for lunch. I harboured with Phillips team up in a small corpse of trees in a valley that led up to the main Cappa to Armagh Road. The satellite patrols harboured up in nearby wood lines or ditches. The soldiers got their mini-issue stoves out and began to brew up. We all dug into our ration packs of Army Biscuits AB with meat spread. The food is pretty awful from our 24-hour ration packs, but we make up for it when we are back at camp.

In Ireland, there are a great many stray dogs that will latch onto army patrols as the lads tend to feed them sweets and biscuits. I try to encourage the soldiers not to feed the dogs as it can be a security hazard. The IRA Patrols and snipers will watch where the dogs are, and they can use them as target identifiers to fire on our otherwise covert patrols. Sadly, in a rural patrol, the dogs are impossible to control or get rid of. Phillip was very disciplined with his team and kept the dogs at bay, but he did seem to have an affinity with the myriad of crows we have in Ireland and would often be seen feeding the birds. The Crows which are normally such cautious birds remarkably appeared to have no fear of Phillip at all. That day was no different and I could see Phillips across the valley sitting slightly apart from his men quietly feeding a couple of crows with bits of biscuit he threw towards them.

The voice of Hardwick changed in Tom's head to that of his son Phillip.

"Scouts, get ready to move in five minutes. We need to head north towards the Pick-up point. Scotty, get the lads in their order of March." The soldiers quickly stowed their kit and filed out of the ditch where they had harboured up. Phillips radio crackled into life in his earpiece.

"Ready to move?" came the familiar voice of the Company HQ Signaller.

"Ready," responded Phillip with the other Section Commanders following suit.

"Weather is closing in, boss." The scout turned to Phillip. The familiar black rain clouds were rolling in from the Irish Sea to the south and east up over the Mountains of Morn and beginning to dump their cargo of rain. The whole area was soddened from relentless rain, and it was already beginning to grow dark despite being only 2 pm in the afternoon. *Fun in Sunny December in Ireland,* Phillip thought.

"Let's TAB on, lads, we need to get to the PUP by 1500hrs otherwise we will miss the Heli Lift and it is a long walk in the rain and dark back to HQ."

"Your crows are sticking with you, boss!" The scout grinned pointing at the birds as they flipped from treetop to tree top along the hedge line the patrol were skirting.

"Gives me the fucking creeps, those bastards, why won't you let me shoot the cunts." Flyn the gunner moaned at Phillip from the rear of the patrol. "I have told you all they are a sign of good luck and my dad always said never shoot the crow,"

Phillip retorted to his men winking at Major Hardwick his guest for the day.

The wind was picking up and driving the rain and sleet into the faces of the young soldiers as they toiled up the hill towards the top of the Cappa Moor and the tarmacked road. Phillip could see the three section with young Cpl Bowens familiar figure striding purposefully towards the houses of Cappa village. Phillip aimed his patrol to the left and south point of the village where the road headed high into the moor. There was a culvert under the road there and he wanted to check it. *The culvert would be an ideal hiding point for the Provos to place weapons,* he thought.

"Fuck me, boss, this weather is grim," the scout Pte Rock muttered to Phillip as the patrol waited at the end of the tree line for the other satellite patrols to reach their rendezvous points. "Head for the edge of the village Rocky, Cpl Bowen will go through the centre and 3 Section will be at the rear. 2 Section will be over there to the north, so we cover the right flank and the south. If there are any PIRA in the village, we will cut off their escape. Also, I want to look at the culvert under the speed sign at the edge of the village."

"Rgr that," came the reply from Rocky and they moved away. The wind seemed to be growing in strength as the storm blew in from the sea to their south. The sky grew darker and darker. "The fucking crabs won't be flying in this, boss," shouted Flynn to Phillips rear.

"Shut the fuck up," hissed Phillip. "The RAF are a splendid bunch, and I don't need you calling them fucking Crabs and shouting you brainless mouth off when we are on patrol so shut up you bell end!" Phillip found Private Flynn annoying at the best of times but when out on a wet cold dark moor in a republican area Philip really could not stand the man.

At least the crows had given up. The two companions that had latched onto Philip as soon as the patrol had begun were gone. Blown away by the gale, I assume Phillip absentmindedly thought to himself. Just as well as it gives the lads the creeps. Phillip had always fed crows and rooks on the farm at home as a boy especially as his dad used to recount the time when he believed a crow saved his life in Korea.

Out of nowhere, the crows reappeared, flapping gracelessly as they fought the gathering storm. Both pitch black birds landed on the road sign by the Culvert that Phillip was slowly moving his patrol towards. The two birds crouched down in the wind to make themselves as small and low as possible. Their black unblinking eyes seemed to watch Phillip intently not moving just sitting like two sentinels.

"That's weird, boss," Rocky called back to Phillip, "your pets have returned and are sitting at the RV waiting for us."

Phillip looked up from his sodden map he was trying to read as they moved along. In one arm, he had his SLR or Self Loading Rifle a large, long and heavy cumbersome weapon cradled in front of him as he held his map that the wind was frantically tugging at. The cold grey driving December rain driven from the sea stung his eyes. The wind had grown again in intensity as the four-man team toiled up the hill towards the culvert and the waiting crows.

Phillip could see the other team to his left moving through the wood line towards the moor road and Cappa village. *Not a soul on the road today,* Philip thought. *That's fucking odd, they should all be on the school run down to Dunganon.*

"Sierra One Alpha this is Alpha One," Phillip called up Cpl Bowen on his radio. Rain was running down Phillips neck and into his earpiece. The radio crackled impotently. *Fuck this isn't right,* Phillip thought. *That road should be buzzing with parents.* "One Alpha are you receiving me?" Phillip called again on the small radio on his chest but still no response from Bowen. "Doughty try to raise comms with the company command," Phillip bellowed at the diminutive signaller that was between him and the rear gunner.

"Pick up the pace, Rocky!" Phillip shouted forward to the scout. The soldiers' green combats had turned a grimy brown by the incessant rain and all four of the young men were doubled down walking into the unforgiving wind. "I want us to get to that culvert before the Bowen makes the village, Rocky." *No cars on the road and no lights in the houses as if they are all empty. No movement. There must be something wrong*, Phillip thought.

"Yes, sir," Rocky grunted intent only on getting this godforsaken patrol over with and getting out of the rain. Speed up lads Phillip shouted back at Doughty and Flynn to his rear. Both soldiers shouldering large amounts of kit stared blearily at him squinting through the rain and nodded their acknowledgement. He was a good officer, and they would follow him anywhere despite the rain.

Phillip could see to his left Cpl Bowens Patrol was now getting onto the main road having moved through the thickest part of the hedge. *Good drills*, he thought, Bowen may be young, but he knew to avoid gateways that could so easily be booby trapped. The Section was turning towards to village. We must speed up!

2 Section to Phillips right were still a good kilometre to his rear and barley visible in the driving rain and cloud and the rear section were hidden in the dead ground directly behind Phillip section. *I hope Bowen has got eyes on all of us,* Phillip thought grimly.

"One Section this is Sunray Over."

The crisp upper-class Sandhurst of southern England crackled into life on the inter platoon radio earpiece startling Phillip as the Company HQ called in.

"One Platoon go," Phillip responded. "What's your progress – Over."

"Roger that, we noticed the lack of traffic on the road and the lack of movement in the village? Over."

"Yes, agreed. Something is up. Take Care. Out."

The two crows that had been sitting on the road sign took off as one and were silently carried up by the howling wind. *Like Phantoms,* Phillip thought as he stared momentarily at them. Phillip and his team pushed on covering the last 100 metres to the waiting road and culvert. He signalled to the scout Private Rock to get onto the road with him and cross the bridge to the culvert. The two soldiers to his rear knew their drills well enough and crouched down in the lee of the thick hedgerow with Major Hardwick, next to the road whilst Phillip and Rocky forced a way through the hedge and onto the road. Water was coursing down the black tarmac road down the hill and away from Cappa village.

The wind literally pushed the two men the final few steps towards the sigh and the culvert opening.

There was a roll of thunder out to sea as Rocky crossed the bridge and culvert and went firm in a crouching position on the far side of the road. The remaining two soldiers in the section were now on the road. The radio operator Doughty crouched low next to the road traffic sign now vacated by the two crows. The gunner Flynn was lying prone with his GPMG pointing up the road towards the village. Philip confident that his team was sufficiently positioned walked on to the culvert and looked over the tiny bridge into the greasy grey murk of the ditch below. The rain leaden clouds continued to roll in from the sea and the visibility up on the moor was getting worse. Already dark skies were made all the more grim and forbearing by the mid-winter gloom. Phillip peered hard down into the ditch and then saw the bright plastic drum sticking out above the water line. The barrel was one of the types used by farmers across the province to hold acid used to make silage but this barrel, sticking out of the water and filth in the ditch had clearly been altered for another purpose. There were red and green wires leading out of the barrel and clumsily buried into the bank of the ditch.

"Fuck, a bomb," Phillip hissed to himself. The barrel was standing bolt upright four foot high and as wide as two men. Once commandeered by IRA Bombers, they would be crammed full of explosive and were capable of destroying a house or a convoy of vehicles.

Phillip looked up; time seemed to have slowed down. The rain and wind still pelted him, and he could see the huddled form of Private Rock the scout crouching in a gateway 20 metres to his front. To his rear, his radio operator and gunner were staring at him.

"Move away. Scatter, fucking scatter; there is a bomb!" Phillip screamed at his team frantically waving at his men to move.

The men immediately got to their feet and began to run from their Commander. He was clearly shouting an order to them to spread out, but no sound reached them, all the noise swept away by the howling wind. Suddenly, there was a crackle of machine gun fire. A contact. The noise came up the valley from the rear section. *They must have come across the bomb detonation team,* Phillip thought. He looked down into the culvert and saw a small light flashing on a clock attached to the side of the barrel. He heard the crows calling. That was weird he thought they are back, and he could see them circling overhead battling with the wind. Then there was a blinding flash.

Harding's voice came again into George's head.

Mr Jones, your son was an exceptional man. His actions that day ensured all his section were uninjured but as you know Phillip was killed instantly by the blast our rear section intercepted the IRA Patrol that detonated the bomb. They killed terrorist that detonated the bomb, but the remaining IRA patrol escaped across the Black Water in the south.

I know Phillip left a wife and young son Charlie and the regimental family's officers will already have been in touch with Phillips wife to see how we can support her and young Charlie. I also am aware Phillip had a younger brother Jeremy who I hope will be a support to you at this terrible time. You should be aware Jeremy has already contacted the family's officer to see if there is any compensation owed to your family, but we will only be discussing that with Phillips next of kin.

All that remains for me to do is to once again give you my best wishes and condolences at this terrible time. I will get over to meet you both when we finish our tour here in Ireland in the spring.

Kind Regards,
Major Mark Hardwick
A Company
2nd Battalion Light Infantry.

Chapter 9
Jeremy

The cuckoo squeezed into the crow's nest. There were four eggs nestling in the tight-knit branches and the blue-grey bird quickly laid her egg making the clutch five. The bird knew the crows could not count and quickly vacated the nest leaving the crows her gift. If the bird could smile, it would have been grinning from ear to ear.

George could hear a steady beeping. He felt dry and clean again and could taste the hard smell of detergent. He tried to move but nothing responded. He tried to open his eyes but could not. George was aware of voices around him. "Do not panic, George!" he told himself. He was clearly lying in a bed; it had a dry and clinical feel to it and cold metal rails seemed to be pressing in on his left side. Right, I must be in a hospital bed he reasoned. The voices around him were becoming clearer.

"But George needs to get up now! He can't loll around in bed all day wasting the hospitals time like this!"

That's Rachel, George thought.

"For Christ's sake, Rachel!" A male voice that sounded old and tired. "George has had a stroke."

"That's Idris, what does he mean I have had a stroke?" George could move his eyes but that was it. There was a searing pain across half his body with his left side having a horrible numb and floppy feeling. It felt empty like his jaw used to feel as a child when he was injected with anaesthetic to have a filling in his teeth.

Idris seemed not to see him as he talked across the bed to Rachel and Charlie who had slipped quietly into the tiny room. George could see all of them, but his eyes were blurred, and he felt like he was floating. Moving around the tiny room not anchored to his hospital bed as his wizened frame of a body was. Indeed, he suddenly realised with a jolt he was staring down at himself. Rather than shocked by this, he found himself wondering how on earth did his body become so small and weak. His own eyes peered at himself noting the misty unresponsive blue eyes staring lifelessly back at him.

"That fucking clown of an uncle of yours will be on the move! It will be like the quickening of a werewolf when he hears your grandfather is this ill. The hairs on his back will be standing on end and he will be on his way the idle good for nothing, cunt."

Idris was talking urgently to Charlie by the hospital room door and out of ear shot from Rachel who was sitting next to Charlie in the bed staring vacantly out of the window.

"The Duke?" Charlie asked with a smile to his great uncle. "Tell it like it is Uncle Idris, I haven't seen that fat twat for years ever since Grandad threw him out and off the farm."

"Bollocks!" George was back in his own body in a flash and away from the ceiling just as he was getting comfortable with the idea. "I cannot go and leave Rachel and Charlie to deal with that twat he thought to himself."

A young student nurse came in to check the heart monitors "Gosh his heart rate is much stronger and stabilising, he is a strong man your grandad!" The nurse smiled at Charlie.

"He certainly is that!" Charlie smiled admiring the young woman's slim body through her tight starched white nurse's uniform.

"For Christ's sake, Charlie," Idris muttered under his breath.

"I am off to get a coffee, come on Rachel." Rachel silently got up and followed Idris and the young nurse from the room.

Charlie pulled up one of the large wooden hospital armchairs and sat thoughtfully by his comatose grandfather. The old man's eyes were slightly open, and Charlie wondered to himself if George could see anything. He took Charlie's wizened and frail hand in his own. "When did your hands get so small, Pops? I always remember them as great paws when I was a kid. You used to say they smelt of dead men! And you were going to leave them to me lacquered as a pair of ash trays!"

Gripping the old man's hands gently, Charlie began to think about his erstwhile Uncle, his dead father's brother the infamous Jeremy. For years, nicknamed the Duke by Idris because of his massive level of self-entitlement. Charlie had never been able to think of him or call him Uncle due to the unbearable way he had behaved towards Charlie's long dead mother and his beloved grandparents Rachel and George.

"Idris thinks the Duke will be coming back from France, Grandad! I hope all the French sun has made him a kinder man. It must be ten years since I have seen him," Charlie mused more to himself than his comatose grandfather.

George eyes were barely open, but he could hear Charlie talking but it felt like the lad was miles away. The Duke Jeremy was on his way back to gloat at his father's crippled form.

Chapter 10
2004 The Tsunami

For once up in the hills around the farm, it was a white Christmas. The young teenager Charlie thought this was fantastic and he loved every minute of it. It was Boxing Day and there was a heavy frost on the ground which crackled underfoot as Charlie walked down to the cattle shed which steamed in the pre-dawn gloom. The young man had a lot on his mind, he had finally convinced his grandparents that the farming life was not for him yet and he wanted to see the world. Charlie had decided to follow in his father's footsteps and join the army. Charlie's mum had been so heart broken by the death of Pa Philip as Charlie called the father, he never knew that she withered away over the years becoming a recluse on the farm and dying of cancer when Charlie was five. Grandpa George and Nanny Rachel had been wonderful throughout whilst Charlie and his mum lived in a cottage on the farm but despite this his mum faded away.

Grandpa George had his own problems with the ever obnoxious Uncle Jerry, Phillip's older brother, who despised his nephew Charlie and his bereft mother. Charlie could never get his head around this but had given up trying to understand. One of Charlie's mates at sixth form Becky had been studying psychology and had told him that people were either mad, bad or sad. Charlie had decided that Uncle Jeremy was a mixture of all three but mostly bad.

Boleck had told Charlie that when his father had been killed there was not a shred of emotion from Jeremy at either the funeral or any time after. Charlie always remembered Jeremy as a weak grey man with pallid toad like skin and lank greasy hair who seemingly and secretly delighted that his younger brother the wonderful Phillip was safely dead and out of the way so that Jeremy could inherit the farm and all his parents' attention which he so clearly craved. That was until baby Charlie and his mum arrived from the family quarters in Andover and took up residence on the farm much to Jeremy's fury and disgust.

Jeremy's campaign against Charlie and his mum began immediately upon their arrival. The relentless sneering and accusations of gold digging laid against Charlie's mum had done nothing to help the emotionally crippled woman or help her through her crushing grief for Philip. Despite having baby Charlie to care for, she fell further and further into depression, listlessness and hopelessness.

Charlie was mulling this all over as he walked to the cattle shed. Old Boleck had beaten him to it though, now in his early 80s, he was to Charlie's amazement still going strong and although officially retired he lived in one of the converted barns and worked part time for George.

"Good morning, young Charlie, and a happy Boxing Day to you!"

Although with a thick Polish accent Boleck's English was faultless. "Where is your lovely Uncle Jeremy? I thought it was his turn to milk this fine morning," Boleck continued with a grin. His voice was laced with sarcasm and an unfamiliar look of anger hovered behind his coal dark eyes. Although Boleck was undeniably old he still cut a very foreboding figure and had always retained his physical strength. He still stood at 6 feet tall with muscles of a man in his fifty's not in his eighties. *I would not like to meet this man in a dark alley,* Charlie thought to himself.

"Anyway, how was your Christmas, my young friend?" Boleck smiled at the 18-year-old. They fell into step with each other and walked down to the cattle shed where, still in darkness the cows had become alerted to their approach and had begun to low and moo excitedly at the anticipation of being fed and relieved of their heavy burdens of milk.

As you know, I have my niece Ania over with her husband. I think they plan to move here and settle in Birmingham now Poland is a member of the EU. Ahh the brave new world. Charlie smiled at his old friend as he opened the gate to the shed and the cows began to spill out into the collecting yard keen to get to the milking parlour and their breakfast.

The same Alpha group of lead cows would always push to the front of the herd and be the first group through the milking parlour and back to the comfort of the cattle shed leaving the older and weaker animals to bring up the rear of the group.

Boleck and Charlie entered the dark milking parlour. "Christmas was okay, Boleck, but Jeremy did get really drunk and nasty to Grandad and Nanny again. He went to the Red Lion on a bender of Christmas Eve. When he finally came home, it was getting light and I got on with the milking with Grandad. Uncle Jeremy didn't then surface until lunchtime yesterday and as you can imagine he was no fun to be around. The day was frankly a bit miserable with just me, him and Nan and Grandad."

"Your grandfather does not need that shit neither does your Nan!"

Boleck growled as he went to get the milk filters ready to start the milk pump. Charlie busied himself with connecting the pipes to the milk tank that had been left to drain overnight. The older man fished around in a red bucket on the concrete floor in the corner of the dairy and fished out the brightly coloured plastic discs that contained the four consecutively smaller metal filters that would filter the milk as it made its way to the Bulk tank. He deftly pulled them from the acid inside the red bucket, swilled them off and clicked them into place as he had done countless times before.

The dairy was a small brick room leading off from the milking parlour. The whole building was a long concrete and brick shed that was open to the collecting yard at one end where the cows were milling impatiently around. Inside the parlour, the cows would walk up either side of the wall whist the two men stood in a pit in the centre of the building placing the milking clusters of four suckers onto each group of eight cows as they entered the parlour. The men worked with an automatic grace, Charlie had been working in this parlour pit since he was three and had no fear of the large lumbering cows that would occasionally thrash out with their hind legs as the cow man worked along the line.

Moving along the lines of cows relentlessly removing the clusters of metal and rubber from the cow's udders when they were done and send the cows relieved of their loads on their way to make space for the next group of eight cows gleefully entering the parlour for their corn and relief. Conversation dropped to a minimum due to the relentless droning sound of the milking machine and the mooing and grumbling of the cows. Radio Four burbled on in the background telling the two men that the Queen had been to Sandringham for Christmas and that it was snowing in Scottish Highlands.

After two hours of hard work dodging cow muck as it sprayed from some of the beasts and the occasional cow shit missile was coughed from the rear of a particularly large bovine flying across the parlour and missing Charlie's head by an inch the men completed the twice daily routine and all the cows were milked and happily ensconced back inside their sheds. The last cow (number 5 freeze branded on her hind) known as Ruby hobbled away on her ancient (in cow years) legs back to the comfort of her stall.

"So anyway," Charlie resumed where he had left off two hours earlier. "Jeremy comes back drunk from the pub sleeps till midday, misses the Christmas Service at St Anne's, which as you can imagine really upset Nan and Grandad and then slouches down for lunch. He was totally silent during the meal, didn't say Happy Christmas or anything and got no presents for anyone despite the fact that I bought him a bottle of scotch and Nan and Grandad gave him a load of cash. It was as much as I could do to keep my mouth shut. You could have cut the atmosphere with a knife. Nan silently gave Jeremy his roast turkey and we all ate in silence! Great fun!

"After lunch, Nan went to get Jeremy his presents, I had already exchanged presents with Nan and Grandad before church. They gave him a £1000 which I thought was really generous but that ungrateful shit just looked at the money and said is that it! And with that, he went back to his room. It is not like he does anything to earn it or be a reliable help on the farm. So that was pretty much the entire day, after Jeremy had skulked back to his room, I played Risk with Grandad and watched TV till it was time to milk the cows again at 5. I then went over to see my new girlfriend Laura at her mum and dad's in the evening and was bloody relieved to get out of the house for a bit. Are you coming up for some breakfast at the house? I know that Nan is expecting you and we would all be relieved for the company as Jeremy is such a royal pain in the arse around you. I think he is scared of you!"

"Yes, of course." Boleck grinned. "I always have breakfast with your nan and grandad on Boxing Day, it is our little tradition! Ania and her boyfriend won't be up yet, so I am in no rush. I always find your Uncle Jeremy very entertaining, he is so. How do you say in English? Self-Righteous and self-entitled like a little eight-year-old boy trapped in a man's body!"

The hot and cold auto washes of the Milking system had completed their runs and the diary and milking parlour smelt strongly detergent; the cows were content in their cattle shed feeding on the silage that George had quietly been putting out with the tractor whilst the two men milked. George had scrapped the yard and sheds clear of cow muck with the old red Fergusson tractor whilst the cows had been out of the way being milked.

"Hey, you two," George called Boleck and Charlie as they emerged from the diary, "Charlie your Nan is frying Black pudding and bacon for you and Boleck! Come on, let's go and fill our boots!"

The two old men and the teenager piled into the hot kitchen where the sound of hot fat crackling in the saucepan was accompanied by the radio playing Carols from Kings College on repeat from the day before. Rachel, now well into her sixties with hair scrapped back grinned at the three as she stood at the stove turning the black pudding over in the pan. "You three absolutely stink of cow muck! Go and strip those overall off, the three of you! Happy belated Christmas to you, Boleck, by the way and how is that lovely niece of your and her boyfriend?"

"Still in bed I expect, Rachel, my cottage is a house of ill repute! They plan to move to Birmingham in the New Year and get jobs. I have no idea what doing but they are both very bright, so I am not too worried." The men stripped off their overalls and Wellingtons in the wash house with the door to the kitchen ajar scrubbing their hands and faces as Rachel looked on with maternal approval. When they had finally cleared the last of the cow muck from their nails Rachel inspected all of their hands and allowed them access to the kitchen where they gathered around the kitchen table.

Boleck gazed wistfully around the kitchen, although he often came into the house it was normally for a hurried coffee or to grab some forms for the cattle. The Boxing Day breakfast was always fun and a chance to relax with George and Rachel and of course young Charlie who he had watched grow up. There was often Jeremy too, angrily bumping around the house like a spectre at the feast. The Kitchen had hardly changed in the 60 years he had been at the farm, he remembered first arriving from Poland in 1942 little more than a boy himself at 18 and not much older than Charlie is now but already aged by the things he had seen back home. So many people had come and gone in those 60 years, Ruby had long since passed and Tommy only outlived her by a couple of years withering away after Phillip had been killed in Ireland. Boleck thought the shock of losing Phillip had killed Ruby out right. The horror of losing her beloved grandson like that had brought memories of her own brother's death at Dunkirk so many years before. Ruby's death had been a quick one, she had been found dead in the green house of a suspected heart attack while she was harvesting her tomatoes. With Ruby gone, Tommy withered away. Once such a strong horse of a man with arms like pistons he shrank away. George and Rachel did their best to keep his spirits up, moved him back to the main farmhouse but he would sit silently for hours staring out across the farm towards the spire of St Anne's church in the distance. It was as though he had lost his son and not George and Rachel.

After six months, Tommy's weight had dropped so dramatically that Charlie persuaded him to go to the doctor in the village. The doctor quickly diagnosed cancer of the stomach and that was the last straw for Tommy who visibly gave up, refused any treatment and died within a month. Boleck remembered being bereft, Tommy had always been a father figure to him and had given him a home when he needed it most. Boleck was horrified by the lack of weight of Tommy's coffin when he had acted as one of the pall bearers. How could this once massive man weigh so little the ravages of cancer had eaten him up?

The door burst open and broke Boleck's daydream and Jeremy sauntered in scowling sulkily at his parents and at Boleck. Despite being well into his thirties, he still had the air of an arrogant and petulant teenager. At over six feet tall, he loved nothing more than to try a intimidate people with his height and ever-increasing bulk as middle age spread claimed him prematurely. Boleck noticed Jeremy must have put on another stone in the last few months and now sported a large beer gut that sagged wobbling and white over his belt and clearly visible below his shirt. So different to his trim and fit parents.

Jeremy was also allowing his lank greasy blonde hair to grow long and for reasons known only to himself he had begun to grow a beard that was patchy and ginger and did little to cover his growing double chin. Boleck mused to himself that Jeremy had begun to look like some evil drunk Santa that had gone off the rails.

Jeremy slumped into one of the wooden captain's chairs at the end of the kitchen table. The chair groaned and sagged alarmingly under his weight. "Eggs please, mother," he commanded his mother who stood rigid at the stove. All the earlier good humour in the room had evaporated to be replaced by an awkward silence.

"I have a blinding hang over and before you both ask, I am not working on the farm while I am over as I have a lot of work and calls to make around my new modelling agency. In the New Year, I have a young Latvian girl coming over to do a photo shoot, maybe you could talk to her for me Boleck, Latvia is in your neck of the woods is it not." Jeremy stared patronisingly at the elderly man who was old enough to be his grandfather.

"Not really, Jeremy. I am from Poland and speak Polish, Latvia is a totally different country." Both George and Rachel were visibly gritting their teeth whilst young Charlie was doing his best not to laugh out loud staring out of the window incredulous at his hated uncle's lack of self-awareness. Meanwhile undeterred, Jeremy continued to hold forth completely unaware of the frosty silence that had enveloped the room.

"Yes, I plan to set up a number of photo shoots on the farm whilst I am here, I need some winter scenes. Boleck I am starting a new magazine, it will be a ground breaker and I am calling it the Sex Express!"

Rachel dropped the frying pan with a clatter and turned to stare at her hefty and hairy son. "You are doing what?" she hissed.

"Mother, you could not possibly understand. It will be artistic and is all the rage in London. I will make a fortune! Father, I will need more money before I go back 'to town' that's what we call London, Boleck, for my flat rent and expenses."

Jeremy just rattled on and on like his personal internal radio was on permanent send as we used to say in the War Boleck thought to himself. George meanwhile said nothing but slowly lifted the Framers Weekly that he had hurriedly picked up when Jeremy had begun his monolog higher to cover his eyes as off to study some very interesting article about Ayrshire Bull semen on America. Rachel had collected the frying pan from the floor that had mercifully been empty and continued to angrily bang around the kitchen smashing eggs into the fryer. Clearly getting no response from his parents, Jeremy turned to Charlie and Boleck. "You chaps missed a treat not having any of my home-made beer last night. I think it has real promise. I will thinking of naming it," mumbles Frown. "Charlie, what do you think?"

"Not sure." Charlie grinned. "I think it has a unique taste." It was Boleck's turn to stifle a laugh as Jeremy engaged with a clearly squirming and uncomfortable Charlie who was biting his lip so hard it looked like it might bleed. *The stuff tastes like cat's piss mixed with toilet cleaner,* Boleck thought to himself.

"Yes, if the modelling and the Sex Express do not take off, I think I have a definitive future as a Master Brewer," Jeremy announced airily to the room.

"Here are your eggs on toast," Rachel said as she moved silently across the room.

"Oh, for fuck's sake, mother, who on earth taught you to cook eggs? These eggs are overdone and disgusting!" George's farmers weekly shot up even further totally obscuring the old man's face whilst Boleck and Charlie shot each other horrified looks. Rachel turned on a sixpence moved in total silence but a quiet intensity that scared Charlie to death and stood behind Jeremy. She then leant over his shoulder scooped up the eggs with her hands and slapped them onto his head where she rubbed the eggy, buttery mass into his already greasy scalp.

"There you go, you arrogant little shit, now get out of my kitchen." Jeremy let out a howl of surprise and leapt to his feet. "Have you gone mad!" but quickly retreated in front of the wrath of his mother and scuttled from the room. Boleck began to clap slowly grinning at Rachel who with a red face had returned to the sink to wash her hands. Charlie began clapping too and George emerged from his farmers weekly and went to Rachel's side. "And you can fuck off too, you weak old man, what use are you? You never get a grip of Jeremy and now we have a nightmare on our hands!" Boleck and Charlie took this as a cue and began to quietly leave the room in Jeremy's wake leaving behind their cooked breakfast. The radio cut across the room.

"This is a news flash: Reports are coming in of a large Tidal wave or tsunami that has engulfed islands in the Indian Ocean."

Chapter 11
Journey's End

As the Magpie is seen as the thief of the forest always on the look out to steal bright things to furnish its nest or to steal eggs from other birds' nests, the brightly coloured Jay who is the smallest member of the Corvid family is known as the watchman of the forest ready to alert all to danger with its loud call and flash of its beautiful plumage.

George had been home at the farm for a month, whilst the log burner was burning brightly in the corner of the kitchen the winter chill had given way to a spring warmth and light that he welcomed. The hospital had released him home into the care of young Charlie and Idris and to George's delight Charlie had started to go out with the very attractive young nurse who had cared for him on the ward (called Clair). Clair was now a regular visitor to Horton and had ensured Charlie and Idris took proper care of old George. Poor Rachel had been properly diagnosed with dementia and had been placed in respite care whilst George settled at home with care staff. Rachel no longer knew who George was and often called him Dad mistaking him for her long-dead father.

Idris had moved into the big house with his younger brother and the two old men kept each other company as the days grew longer into spring. Charlie returned to his Army Unit but was a far more frequent visitor now that he was regularly seeing young Clair and had plans to leave the Army and move home and finally settle down. This really cheered the two old boys. "The Duke." Jeremy had been put to go by a concerted effort of both Idris and Charlie who blocked his access to both of his parents at the hospital. Jeremy who was now at least 20 stone and had long given up daily hygiene had arrived only to immediately begin demanding money for his travel and demanding to see the Will whilst neither of his parents had actually died. This played straight into the hands of the hospital staff who were rightfully horrified by the evil greed of the man and agreed with Idris and Charlie to block access to the vulnerable couple.

When he found out that he was neither a Power of Attorney, Executor or Trustee, he realised the game was up and slunk away back to his lair in France cursing both Charlie and his uncle Idris even accusing Charlie of infecting his grandmother Rachel with Dementia. All they ever heard from Jeremy now was that he was making regular complaints to the Police and other public authorities about George's and Rachel's care and alleged abuse by Idris and Charlie and latterly Clair, towards both Rachel and George. It did not take long for all the agencies to realise these were vexatious complaints and Jeremy became routinely ignored screaming into the void in France. Last heard of he was being deported by a clearly exasperated French government who must have decided to use Brexit as a great pretence to send back this less than useful British export. Apart from an amusing report that

Jeremy had had a fight with the Ferry piano player on his return voyage from France via a friend who happened to be on the same ferry, the family never found out as to why Jeremy was deported but as no one heard from him it was felt best left.

The old crow soared high over the farmhouse chimneys and the old oaks that had been planted to celebrate the victory of Waterloo over two hundred years earlier. His work was done, his family secure and well provided for. He had protected them as best as he could and whilst not always perfect, he had done the best he could. He turned to the blazing sun and kept flying into the light.

END